The Conspiracy

I scanned my father's face. Had he become a Controller yet? Stupid. I didn't know. Couldn't know. It's not as if Controllers go around twitching or exchanging Yeerk high fives or playing with their ears. A Controller looks, acts, seems exactly normal.

My father could be my father. Or he could be screaming, helpless, just beginning to realize that his eyes and ears and mouth no longer belonged to him. . .

Even the book morphs!
Flip the pages
and check it out!

Look for other ANIMORPHS titles
by K.A. Applegate:

1 The Invasion
2 The Visitor
3 The Encounter
4 The Message
5 The Predator
6 The Capture
7 The Stranger
8 The Alien
9 The Secret
10 The Android
11 The Forgotten
12 The Reaction
13 The Change
14 The Unknown
15 The Escape
16 The Warning
17 The Underground
18 The Decision
19 The Departure
20 The Discovery
21 The Threat
22 The Solution
23 The Pretender
24 The Suspicion
25 The Extreme
26 The Attack
27 The Exposed
28 The Experiment
29 The Sickness
30 The Reunion

MEGAMORPHS
1 The Andalite's Gift
2 In the Time of Dinosaurs

ANIMORPHS

The Conspiracy

K.A. Applegate

SCHOLASTIC

Scholastic Children's Books,
Commonwealth House, 1–19 New Oxford Street,
London WC1A 1NU, UK
a division of Scholastic Ltd
London ~ New York ~ Toronto ~ Sydney ~ Auckland
Mexico City ~ New Delhi ~ Hong Kong

First published in the USA by Scholastic Inc., 1999
First published in the UK by Scholastic Ltd, 2000

ISBN 0 439 99602 3

Printed by Cox & Wyman Ltd, Reading, Berks.

10 9 8 7 6 5 4 3 2 1

The author wishes to thank Laura Battyanyi-Wiess for her help in preparing this manuscript.

For Bill Battyanyi

For Michael and Jake

Chapter 1

My name is Jake.

Just Jake.

My last name doesn't matter.

Where I live and go to school don't matter, either.

What matters is that we're in a war, fighting for the survival of the human race.

You're thinking *Yeah, right*. That's OK. I know — I probably would have said the same thing once.

No way. Not a chance. If it's true, then where are the troops storming the beaches? Where are the bombs? Where's the battlefield? The RPVs and cruise missiles?

Well, it's not that kind of a war.

The battlefield is wherever we are, we being

my friends and I. We are animal-morphers, given the ability to absorb DNA by touch and then morph into that animal. It's an incredible weapon, the kind that both dreams and nightmares are made of.

Ask Tobias, who stayed in his red-tailed hawk morph longer than the two-hour limit and now spends his days catching and eating small mammals.

Or check in with any one of us in the small hours between night and morning, when the nightmares come, the nightmares of twisting bodies and mutating minds.

Like I said, this is not your standard type war.

We're the whole army, the six of us. We get some help from the Chee, but they are incapable of violence, so when it comes to the down and dirty, we're it. Us, alone, against an alien empire that has already terrorized the galaxy.

Yeah, I know. Nice odds.

Most of us learned to fight the hard way in a deadly, on-the-job-training type deal.

But some of us had a head start, like my cousin Rachel, who loves it all. And Ax, whose full name is Aximili-Esgarrouth-Isthill, warrior-cadet and younger brother to Elfangor, the Andalite who gave us the power to morph before he was murdered by Visser Three.

I know, sounds like bull, right? Sounds like maybe I need to spend some time in a rubber room.

But it's true. Every now and then the crazy becomes real.

And this is not a clean war, if there is such a thing. I mean a war like World War II, where thousands saw the wrongs being committed and stood up to correct them. Where you attacked an enemy you could see, an enemy who wore a uniform and came right back at you, guns blazing.

This isn't that kind of war at all.

The Yeerks are more subtle than that. They aren't predators, they're parasites. They don't want to destroy humanity, they don't want to make big piles of bodies, they need our bodies in one piece to continue their invasion.

See, they're basically slugs. Parasites. No arms, no legs, no face. Blind.

That's why they need host bodies.

They slither into your ear, seep into the crevices of your brain, open your memories.

And you're still inside yourself while it's happening, trapped, helpless, begging for the nightmare to end.

Only it's real. And it doesn't end.

You want to warn people and you can't make the words come out. But the Yeerk in your head can hear them. It can hear your pitiful cries,

your impotent threats. It can hear you beg, *Please, please leave me, please get out of my head, please. . .* And it can feel you slowly surrendering even the pretence of resistance.

The Yeerks are everywhere, using their involuntary human hosts to move freely, to recruit new members into their cover organization, called The Sharing, with promises of good, clean, wholesome family fun.

They're the ultimate enemy.

We've identified a few of them, though.

Our assistant principal, Mr Chapman.

My best friend Marco's mother.

My big brother, Tom.

I know how the guys fighting in the Civil War felt, North against South, brother against brother.

Living with the dark, ugly fact that if you met your brother on the battlefield, he would kill you.

Unless you killed him first.

I know the real Tom is still inside himself somewhere, raging against the Yeerk holding him hostage, begging for someone to save him.

I know because I was infested once by the same Yeerk who'd first infested Tom before his body had been turned over to a new Yeerk. I had access to its memories, so I saw how Tom had been dragged, screaming, fighting, and finally pleading, to the Yeerk pool to receive his slug.

I was saved. Tom was not.

But it stays with me, that memory. It always will.

So will the battles. Win, lose, or draw, they're chaotic clashes full of pain and rage. And when the fighting's over and the adrenalin drains away, you're left exhausted and sick, with way too many memories.

My grandpa G — "G" for great-grandpa — told me something once, way before I ever could have understood what he'd meant.

My family had driven for eight hours to visit him in his cabin in the woods. He and I were sitting on the dock at the lake, watching the fish snatch mosquitoes off the water's glassy, mirrored surface.

And it was so quiet.

Quiet enough to make me wish I was home with the TV blasting and my dog Homer gnawing on a rawhide chew.

I was about to leave when Grandpa G said, "You know, I see myself in you, Jake. You've got an old soul."

An old soul? Was that supposed to be good or bad?

He never said. Just gave me a small, kind of sad smile, and looked back out over the lake.

I hadn't known what he'd meant then, or why he'd said it. I don't know, maybe he saw my future, somehow. Because now I was old. You

see too much pain and destruction, you get old inside. It's one of the by-products of war.

I'm the unofficial leader of the Animorphs. I send us into battle. When things go wrong, when we get hurt or have to run for our lives, that's on me, too.

I'm not complaining. Has to be done. You know? Someone has to make the calls. A good leader has to make tough, informed decisions. Recognize his soldiers' special strengths and use them accordingly. Fight to win with the knowledge that he may die trying.

But most important, a leader won't ask anyone to do anything he wouldn't do himself.

That one came home to haunt me.

Because in three days, my brother Tom was either going to kill or be killed.

And it was up to me to decide.

Chapter 2

I came round the corner after school and saw a taxi parked out in front of my house.

My mother shot across the porch, suitcase banging against her knees, and hurried down the pavement to the cab.

What the. . . ?

My mum didn't take cabs. Nobody round here did.

Everybody had cars.

"Mum!" I yelled, jogging over. "What happened?"

Because something had definitely happened.

I mean, I've seen my mum sniffle at Save the Children ads and Hallmark cards, but I can't remember the last time I ever saw her really cry.

But she was crying now.

Something must have happened to Tom.

Or to my dad.

My knees went weak and wobbly.

Funny, how even when your whole life has shifted into a daily *Twilight Zone* episode, there are still some things that can make you panic.

"I left you a note on the fridge, Jake," she said, hefting her suitcase into the boot and slamming it shut. "My flight leaves in an hour and the traffic—"

"Mum, *what happened*?" I blurted.

My voice was high and shrill, not exactly the voice of a fearless leader, as Marco would have pointed out, had he been there.

"Oh." She blinked away fresh tears. "Grandpa G died. His housekeeper, Mrs Molloy, found him this morning. I'm meeting your grandparents and we're driving out to Grandpa G's cabin to make the funeral arrangements."

"Grandpa G's dead?" I echoed, trying to wade through the emotions whirling around in my head.

Grandpa G. Not Tom. Not my father.

"Yes. His poor heart just gave out," she said.

"You're going to the cabin?" I said. "What about us?"

"You'll be coming out as soon as your father clears his work schedule," she said, touching my shoulder, forcing a brief smile, and sliding into the backseat. "He'll tell you about it.

Everything will be fine. Make sure your suit is clean. I'll call when I get to Grandma's. I've got to go, honey."

She slammed the door and waved.

I watched as the cab disappeared round the corner.

Now what?

I headed into the house. Checked the scrawled note stuck under an apple magnet on the fridge.

Yeah. Grandpa G was dead.

According to Mrs Molloy, who'd talked to the doctor, his heart had stopped while he was putting jam on a slice of toast. He'd never even got a chance to eat it.

I shivered.

I'd cared about Grandpa G and now he was gone, and my family was smaller.

I didn't like that.

The kitchen door burst open. Tom stormed into the room.

"And I'm telling you, Dad, I can't go!" he snapped, tossing his books on to the table and scowling at me. "What're you looking at?"

"You're home early," I said, surprised.

My father plodded in, weary, harassed, and closed the door behind him.

"So are you," I said, glancing from him to Tom. "Did Mum tell you guys about Grandpa G?"

"Yes," my father said. "I was hoping to get

here in time to take her to the airport but the traffic was terrible. I saw Tom walking home and picked him up."

"Did you know we're supposed to go out to the cabin?" Tom demanded, glaring at me like it was somehow my fault.

"Uh, yeah," I said cautiously, trying to work out what his problem was. "So?"

"So, Tom's already informed me that he doesn't want to leave his friends to attend his great-grandfather's funeral," my father said, looking at Tom, not me. "However, he doesn't have a choice. We're going. All of us."

"When?" I said, feeling like I was missing something important. It was there but I just couldn't grab it.

"We're driving up on Saturday morning," my father said.

"Dad, I can't," Tom insisted. "The Sharing's expecting me to help out this weekend. I gave them my word!"

"Well, you'll just have to explain that something more important came up," my father said. "I thought The Sharing was about promoting family values, right? Well, we're going to pay our respects to Grandpa G as a family."

"Dad, you don't understand!" Tom argued desperately.

Why was Tom so dead set against going out to the lake?

OK, so it was boring. Grandpa G's cabin was the only house on the lake. His closest neighbour had been Mrs Molloy and she lived ten kilometres away, halfway to town.

The only other house around was an old, abandoned hunting lodge across the lake.

No cable. No McDonald's. No streetlights or crowds.

No movies. No malls. . .

No Sharing. No Yeerks. . .

"Uh, Dad?" I said. "How long are we staying?"

"It depends on the funeral. I'll write notes so you'll be excused from school until Tuesday of next week—"

"What?" Tom's eyes bulged in shock. "Tuesday? Dad, no way! Four days? I can't stay away for four days!"

"You can and you will," my father said, losing his patience. "We're going as a family and that's final."

Tom's throat worked. His hands clenched into fists.

And for one brief second I had the crazy thought that he was going to attack my father.

And oh, man, even though I couldn't morph in front of them, I could feel the surge of adrenalin that comes right before a fight.

Three, maybe four days. The maximum time a Yeerk can last without a trip to a Yeerk pool is

three days. Four days without Kandrona rays and the Yeerk in Tom's head would starve.

Starve, Yeerk. Starve!

"It won't be that bad, Tom," I heard myself pipe up. "The lake's nice, remember?"

It broke the stalemate.

Tom looked at me. "You're an idiot, you know that?"

He was playing his role as condescending big brother. I was playing my role, too.

Starve, Yeerk. Die in agony, die screaming, Yeerk!

"Shut up," I said. "I'm not the one who's being a big baby about leaving."

I said it to annoy him and to bring us back to the rhythm we knew, the kind of normal sniping I could handle.

Because the hatred in Tom's eyes when he'd looked at my father had scared me.

And the hatred that had flared up in me, the hatred of the Yeerk, the sick thrill of anticipating its pain, had scared me, too.

"That's because you have no life," Tom sneered.

"Oh, right, and you do?" I shot back.

"More than you'll ever know," he said darkly, distracted now.

"Enough," my father said. "I'm going to change. When I get back we'll order pizza. How does that sound?"

"I'm not hungry," Tom muttered, staring at the floor.

I wasn't either but my father was looking at me expectantly, so I said, "Pizza. I'm there."

My father nodded, satisfied, and left.

I gave my brother a look of sympathy, making peace. "Maybe you can get out of it, some way."

I had to fight to keep the sneer off my face. *Or maybe, Yeerk, your cover is falling apart, maybe you'll have to choose between keeping Tom and keeping your filthy life.*

"Shut up," Tom said absentmindedly. The Yeerk had no use for me, no interest in me. I was dismissed. Irrelevant.

I turned and blasted out into the back garden, my mind already buzzing with the possibilities.

Tom's Yeerk was trapped. Under pressure. Squeezed. It wasn't ready for this turn of events. Didn't know how to play it out. Didn't know what to do.

An opportunity? Maybe. Yeah, maybe.

Die, Yeerk!

Chapter 3

Supper was awful.

Tom tried everything to get out of going.

He begged. Pleaded. Complained. Sulked.

He even tried reasoning.

My father didn't budge.

I finished supper and bolted. I needed to think about what was going to happen and I couldn't do it with Tom around.

I hit the street, automatically heading for Marco's, but I really didn't know where I was going.

I wanted to talk to Cassie, but she and her parents, both vets, were at some animal rescue seminar until later.

Too bad, too, because she was the one I really wanted to talk to.

Out of all of us, Cassie's the one who really understands the more complicated things: motives, emotions, right and wrong.

Marco's my best friend, and if I wanted to talk about what works, about how to get from point A to point B and forget the consequences, I'd talk to Marco.

But Cassie sees beneath the surface. I'm no genius, but I knew I was too close to this to see clearly.

"Yo, Jake man! I was just on my way over to your house." Marco. Jogging towards me. "I need your English notes."

I looked up, startled. "Oh. Uh, hi."

"What'd I do, wake you up?" he said, body-checking me.

I shoved him back. "Since when did you start saying 'Yo'?"

"I was going to yell 'Hey, handsome,' but I thought you might prefer 'Yo'."

"Uh-huh."

"So, yo-yo, what's up?"

"I was just thinking about something," I said, shrugging. Then I decided what the heck. Marco's been my friend since we were in the sandpit. Plus, he'd lost his mum — complicated story — so I reckoned he'd know how I felt. "My Grandpa G died today."

"Man. Too bad," he said, falling in beside me as we headed back to my house. "He was

old, though, right? I mean he was in World War III."

"World War II, Marco. Two."

"No, duh," he said. "We spent a really unpleasant afternoon in the middle of World War II, you may recall. Or at least some time-distorted version of World War II."

Long story there, too.

"Yeah, he was in the war. The real war," I said as we rounded the corner to my house. "My mother flew out to help with the funeral arrangements. We're supposed to—"

My father's car wasn't in the driveway.

Odd.

"When's the funeral?" Marco said.

"I'm not sure. Probably Monday," I said, walking a little faster. The deep, dark part of my brain, the part that sensed danger, was already dumping adrenalin into my blood.

Something wasn't right.

"What?" Marco asked, instantly catching my mood.

"Don't know. A feeling."

A feeling like there was something important I'd forgotten. And because I had forgotten it. . .

I tried to shake it off. I walked faster. "I'll be out of school on Monday. Maybe Tuesday too," I said absently, crossing the front lawn. "Me, my dad and Tom are driving out on Saturday morning."

"That's what, four days?" Marco said, then grabbed my arm. "Four days without Kandrona rays?" he said in a low, tense voice. "Does Tom know how long you're going to be gone?"

"Yeah, he and my dad had a big fight about it," I said, tugging free. "My dad said he had to go."

And then Tom had looked at my father with black hatred.

No, not Tom. The Yeerk inside him.

Controlling him.

Tom's hands, doubled into fists.

Poised to leap at my father.

"You left them alone," Marco said. Not an accusation. No blame. Just fact.

Like I said, Marco sees the line that goes from A to B. He'd already seen Tom's dilemma. And he'd seen Tom's ruthless solution.

I followed Marco's narrowed gaze.

My house was still.

Too still.

I bolted, stumbled up the steps, and threw the door open with a slam that echoed down the street.

Chapter 4

Silence.

The empty kind, when you know nobody's there but you.

"Dad?" I yelled anyway, running into the hallway. "Dad? Tom?"

No answer.

Heart pounding, I took the stairs two at a time.

"Dad?"

Looked in my parents' bedroom. In Tom's. In mine.

Neat — except for my room. Empty.

Which made me feel a little better, but not much.

"Jake," Marco said from right behind me.

"Yaaahh!" I yelped, going airborne.

"Sorry."

"Don't do that!" I said harshly, pushing past him and heading back down the stairs to the kitchen.

I swung around, searching the kitchen for something, anything that would tell me where they'd gone.

Cabinets. Sink. Glass jars full of cookies and pasta and coffee, lined up on the counter. Coffee machine. Refrigerator. Toaster.

Orderly. Nothing out of place.

I exploded.

Slammed against the side of the refrigerator.

BAM!

One of the magnets fell off. The apple, which had been holding my mother's note about Grandpa G.

Only the second note, the one that had been tacked beneath it, was gone. Had someone taken it? Why, when it had the flight number and details about what to bring when we drove out?

The rubbish.

Frantically, I grabbed the plastic bin and flipped open the lid. Knelt and peered inside.

Lying crumpled atop the banana skins and the coffee grounds and the empty yogurt container was a wad of pink paper. Crumpled. I rose and smoothed it out on the counter.

The top of the note was the one from my

mother with the flight information. At the bottom of that note was my father's handwriting.

Jake: Went to a Sharing meeting with Tom to explain why he can't help them out this weekend.
Be back soon.
Love, Dad.

"Oh, God," I whispered.

My father hadn't thrown away the note. Tom had. He'd been covering his tracks.

Tom was taking my father to The Sharing.

But not so he could be excused from his obligations.

He was going to make our father a Controller. He would watch as they forced him to his knees and pushed his head down into the thick, sludgy Yeerk pool. He would listen to his pleas. Listen to his cries. His screams of horror and disbelief and panic. Listen and laugh.

No.

I started to shake.

I should have known. Should have seen it sooner. Marco had seen it, why hadn't I?

"We have to find them," I said, searching my mind frantically for a way to do it.

"How?" Marco said. "We don't even know where they are."

"Marco, this is *my father*!" I shouted, losing it. "I'm not letting them take him."

"Even if we find him, you may not have anything to say about it," he said quietly. "It might already be too late."

No, it couldn't be too late. Couldn't. . .

No. They wouldn't have my father. I was going to stop them. Even if it meant stopping my brother.

Any way I had to.

Marco re-crumpled the note and put it back in the trash.

Placed the apple magnet back on the fridge.

I stood there, frantic, vibrating with impatience, wanting to go, go, GO somewhere, anywhere, just *get going* and find my father.

"We have to cover our tracks, Jake," he explained. "We can't let Tom know that we know."

"Right, whatever," I said, hurrying towards the door.

I didn't tell Marco, but at that moment I just didn't care about keeping our secrets. I didn't care about saving the world. I was saving one man. The rest of the world could take care of itself.

There were some losses I wasn't willing to take, no matter what. I'd lost my brother. That was it. I wasn't losing anyone else.

"The Chee," I said suddenly.

I reached for the phone. Marco pushed the receiver back down. "Not from the house, man. Look. Jake. Jake, listen to me."

"What? WHAT?"

"You're the boss, Jake. You're the fearless leader. But not right now, OK? You're too messed up over this. Let me call the shots."

I knew he was right. I said nothing. I hated Marco right then. Hated him because he wouldn't have made the mistake I'd made. He would have seen. . .

Hated him because he'd already lost his mother and he knew what the inside of my head was like, because he knew I was scared and just wanted to cry.

"Come on, man," Marco said.

We went down the block to a payphone to call Erek King. He's a Chee.

The Chee are a race of androids. Pacifist by design. But definitely anti-Yeerk. The ultimate spies. Our friends. At least as much as a nearly eternal machine can ever be a friend to a weak, short-lived human.

The Chee would know of any Sharing meetings scheduled.

"There's nothing scheduled," the human-sounding voice said.

"But there has to be," I said desperately, pacing the length of the stupidly short phone cord. "Tom's taking my father to it! C'mon, Erek, please!"

"Jake, you know I would tell you if I knew," Erek said with calm regret. "Perhaps Tom asked for an emergency meeting to deal with this problem."

"Then how are we ever going to find out where they are?" I said, glancing at Marco to see if he had any suggestions.

He shrugged, looking miserable.

I turned away, wanting to cry.

Fighting to get hold of myself.

Think, Jake.

If the Chee didn't know where the Yeerks were gathering, how were we supposed to know?

"Wait," I blurted. "Stupid! I don't have to find the Yeerks to find my father. All I have to do is find my father and we'll find the meeting. Should have thought of it."

"All right," Erek said cautiously.

"No, it's easy. He always carries a mobile phone. I'll just call and ask him—"

"You can't," Marco and Erek both said at the same time.

"Why not?" I said.

"Jake, if you call and ask your dad where he is, and then the meeting gets broken up by us, don't you think the Yeerks'll put two and two together?"

"I don't care," I said, before I could stop myself.

The sympathy on Marco's face evaporated. "You're not getting me killed to save your father!" he snapped.

"There may be another way," Erek said, interrupting. "Give me the mobile number. You hang up, dial the mobile, and I'll tap into the frequency. You call but don't speak. If your father picks up, I'll analyse the auditory data and we may be able to determine his location."

I didn't look at Marco. Couldn't. "Good. Great." I gave Erek the number, hung up, and dialled my father's mobile number.

It rang once.

Twice.

My hands were shaking.

Marco was staring at me, eyes narrowed. His body was tense, ready to snatch the receiver if I as much as opened my mouth.

I closed my eyes, willing my father to answer.

Praying it wasn't too late.

Chapter 5

"Hello?"

Tom.

Tom had answered my father's mobile.

My mouth opened automatically to respond.

Marco lunged, twisting the phone out of my hand.

Put it to his ear.

Watched me with dark, unreadable eyes.

I didn't move. I couldn't.

Because I couldn't believe what I had almost done.

If I'd said one word, just one, then I'd either have condemned my father to the Yeerk pool or I would have condemned my friends to death.

I couldn't stop shaking.

Couldn't get control.

Marco listened, then hung up the receiver.

"You'd better call Erek back," he said coolly, stepping away from the phone.

I nodded, too embarrassed to even look at him, too worried about my father to say something that would close the distance between us.

"I've analyzed the incoming data from the call and have narrowed it down to four possible locations," Erek said when I called.

"Four!" I blurted. We didn't have time to search four different places! "Where are they?"

"Well, factoring in the frequency strength, the mobile phone towers that were activated, and background noise such as the sound of jet engines overhead, car engines moving slowly, human footsteps and various other sounds, our analysis suggests they're in the northern section of town, roughly between the eight thousand and the fourteen thousand blocks north-south, and the six hundred and twelve hundred blocks east-west. An area six blocks by six blocks."

"What's in that area that could hold a meeting, even a small one?" I was grateful. I was also impatient. Frantic.

"Senior Citizen Centre, a small shopping mall with four shops, a small hardware store, and repair garage. Plus, about seventy-five private homes."

I let out a curse. "Homes! We can't search seventy-five homes! Erek, I need more."

"There was a snatch of conversation. Just two words."

"What words?"

" 'Normal hours.' "

"What?"

" 'Normal hours.' Like the last two words of a sentence. Blah, blah, blah, 'normal hours'," Erek said.

I had a sudden flash of him on the other end of the line. Would he be in his true android form, or wreathed in the perfect hologram that let him pass as a normal human kid?

"Eliminate the garage," Marco said. "That'd be noisy. Really noisy. If they're open, that is. Same with the hardware. Nails dropping, paint cans being shaken. . . It's the old folks' home or the shops."

"Or one of seventy-five private homes," I said. "Erek? We need your best guess."

"I don't have—"

"Take a shot!" I yelled.

"The shopping mall. Four shops. Play the odds," Erek said.

"Get hold of Rachel. Get her and the others up there to the other locations."

I slammed down the phone. No time for thank-yous. There'd be thank-yous if we won this race.

"Shops," I told Marco.

"What about the old folks? They'd have a main room. Shops wouldn't."

"'Normal hours.' Sounds like a shop."

"Unless it's about mealtime, or visiting time at the old folks' home," Marco said.

"Let's go," I said.

We jogged back to my house. It was the closest, safest place with no one home.

I stripped off my outer clothing — getting down to bike shorts and a T-shirt. The kind of tight, minimal clothing we can morph in.

I focused my mind on one of the double-helix strands of DNA that swim in my blood.

When I opened my eyes, I was falling. Shrinking. And no matter how many times it had happened before, it still made my stomach lurch.

Smaller and smaller, with the floor racing up to slap me, falling like I'd jumped off a skyscraper.

My skin turned grey and white, mottled. Across the dead grey flesh the Etch-A-Sketch lines of feathers were drawn. An eerie design that suddenly was no drawing but three-dimensional reality.

My eyes slid apart, around my head. Eyes that could read a dictionary from a block away. Raptor eyes. Falcon eyes.

My legs shrivelled, becoming mere sticks. My fingers extended out, bare hollow bone that was quickly covered by feathers. Tail feathers erupted from my behind, down my chest, down my back and stomach.

Marco was undergoing a similar mutation. Morphing. It's what we do. It's our weapon.

He was becoming an osprey, I, a peregrine falcon.

Marco began to say something, but his words were cut short as his mouth and nose melted and stiffened and extended into the wicked, curved beak of an osprey.

My talons sprouted, grew curved and sharp.

<I'll meet you there,> I said.

<No, wait.>

<Marco, I'm faster than you are.>

He hesitated. <Yeah. OK. But Jake?>

<What?!> I snapped.

I expected him to say, "Don't do anything stupid."

<You're not alone, man,> Marco said.

Chapter 6

Peregrine falcon. The fastest animal on Earth. In a dive I could hit three hundred kilometres an hour.

But I was a sprinter, not a marathon-runner. To get to the north end of town I had to soar. Not easy in the evening when the sun has cooled and the concrete no longer steams the air to provide lift for a raptor's wings.

I flew hard, circling for altitude. Marco kept pace at first, but then he fell behind and below.

When you're flying, altitude equals speed. Tobias taught me that. Spend the energy to gain altitude, then you can turn a long trip into a single glide.

I rose and rose, milking every breeze to give lift to my swept-back wings. Up I went. And at last, boiling with impatience, I made gravity my friend.

I could not see my specific target but I could see the area, the neighbourhood. I took aim, whipped my wings, and went into a power glide.

Faster, faster!

The wind tore across my feathers. Around my face. Blearing my eyes. Straining my muscles. One wrong move, one sudden flare of my wings and the speed could snap my shoulders, cripple me, leave me falling helpless to Earth.

I was a racing car driver. One wrong twitch of the wheel and I would spin out of control.

No way to measure my speed, but I was flying faster than I'd ever flown before. The ground raced by. Porch lights and streetlights and bright red tail-lights were long neon trails.

I was outpacing the cars on the highway below. But I was too low. I'd misjudged the angle. In my haste I'd not gone high enough, and now I was too low, skimming the treetops and peaked roofs and telephone wires, blazing, a rocket!

My muscles burned, my heart was a jackhammer, my lungs burned.

I blew across the shopping mall before I even realized I was there. I braked carefully, took a wide turn, and circled back.

A Starbucks. No. Too public.

A knife shop. Closed. Dark.

Computer Renaissance. Open. Bright. A possibility.

An antique shop. Lights on. Half-shades drawn up. Two men walking in past a sign that said CLOSED.

I used the last of my speed to buzz the cars in the car park. The car park was full. My dad's car was there.

I landed in the shadows behind the mall. I began to demorph. How to do it? How to attack and get my dad out? What morph, what creature?

My feet sprouted first, pink and bare and huge.

My eyes straddled my bulging, human nose, which had split away from my shrinking beak.

I shot upwards as my legs thickened and grew.

Hair. Fingers.

My insides gurgled and sloshed sickeningly.

An osprey landed on an overturned crate.

I was fully human. Standing with bare feet on gravel and crumpled cans and scruffy weeds.

I glanced at Marco. He was beginning to demorph.

I began to morph. I felt the powerful, tiger DNA stir in my pulsing blood.

Sharp, gleaming fangs sprouted in my mouth. Claws that could disembowel a bull grew from my fingertips.

<No,> Marco said. <We can't go storming in like the marines, Jake! It's too obvious.>

I was still more human than tiger. The yellow teeth, sabre sharp, made speech clumsy. "I'm koink in!"

<Jake, I will have to try and stop you,> Marco said.

We stared at each other for a long, tense moment. A half tiger and a half osprey.

Marco became fully human. I stopped my morph.

"Look," Marco said finally, quietly. "I know you're freaked but if we make this a rescue mission, we're all dead. All of us. Everyone. The Yeerks aren't idiots. They go after your dad and suddenly the Animorphs attack a minor meeting? They can add two plus two, Jake. You let the Yeerks know who you are, Jake, how is that going to help your father?"

He was right. I knew it but I didn't want to hear it.

"We have to create a distraction. Mess up the meeting but not let them know why," Marco said, as thick, coarse hair began sprouting from his bulging, growing body. "We're going to buy some time and I've got it all planned. Do your falcon morph again. Your eyes will be better than mine."

"But—" I said.

"No buts, Jake," he said. "You know me. You know I've worked it out."

I hesitated, frustrated and not used to being

the one taking orders, but I couldn't deny that he was right.

I was losing my clear thinking and that was dangerous.

Surrendering, I concentrated on the falcon morph.

Marco finished his massive, muscled gorilla morph and waited, standing guard until I was done.

<OK,> I said. <Tick-tock, Marco.>

<Well, Rachel's not here so I suppose it's up to me,> Marco said, knuckle-galloping his way around to the front of the mall. <Let's do it!>

He stepped out into the car park. I flew, watching from above.

My father and my brother were close by. One predator, the other prey. Both, in different ways, in mortal danger.

And if they were to be saved, it was up to Marco. Not me.

Chapter 7

It's funny about gorillas. They're gentle creatures by nature. They don't give you the fear chills you get from the big cats or the bears. Mostly when you see them they're zoned out in some zoo cage.

But they are a whole different animal when they're moving. You see a big gorilla moving fast and you get a sense of just how much power you're looking at.

Human-like? Yes. But like a human who's been built at a truck factory.

Marco walked over to a car.

Grunting, he lifted it up by the rear bumper. Lifted it clear off the ground, back wheels not touching.

And dropped it.

WOOOEEEE! WOOOEEE! WOOOEEE!

I almost laughed. Car alarm!

Marco went to another car. He lifted it. Dropped it. And another. Lift. Drop.

WEEEYOOOP! WEEEYOOOP! WEEEYOOOP!

HONK! HONK! HONK! HONK!

WaaaaAAAAAAaaaaaAAAAAAaaaaaAAAAA!

The night was filled with clanging, screaming, whooping car alarms.

And then a very familiar car. One we both knew.

Chapman's car. Chapman, our assistant principal. A leader of The Sharing. A Controller.

An enemy.

Marco didn't lift Chapman's car. He punched it. He punched the driver's door with a fist the size of a milk jug.

SHHHLUUUUUUEEE! SHHHLUUUUUUEEEE!

Then he crashed a huge, hairy gorilla fist down on the hood of my father's new car.

SPREEET! SPREEET! SPREEET!

<Hey!> I hollered, horrified. <That's our car! My dad's going to have a cow.>

<I hope so,> Marco said. Then with barely suppressed glee, <I believe my work here is done.>

He ran back into the shadows. In five minutes he'd be in the air.

It took approximately eight seconds for the doors of the computer shop, Starbucks and the antique shop to begin spewing out very angry men and women.

Chapman came running from the antique shop.

So did my father, with Tom close behind.

"What the heck happened?"

"Vandals!"

"Lousy kids!"

"This neighbourhood has totally gone to—"

"Call the cops!"

"I'm suing this shopping centre!"

"Look at my door!"

That last was Chapman.

The rest of the Controllers from the antique shop looked uneasy.

I waited, holding my breath, counting the seconds until my father, followed by a furious, scowling Tom, wove through the crowd.

"My car!" my father cried. He practically fell to his knees. "Someone hurt my baby!"

"Mine, too," Chapman said, gazing angrily at the fist-sized dent in his car door. He looked around the street, then nodded at the two big, bulky men who were flanking him.

They split up and started searching the street.

<Chapman's got guys looking for us,> I called to Marco. <Better get out of here.>

<Well, come on, dude,> Marco replied. <I'm in a tree down the street. What're you waiting for?>

<I can't go yet, Marco,> I said. <I have to make sure my father's all right. I have to make sure he's still. . . You know.>

I scanned my father's face. Had he become a Controller yet? Stupid. I didn't know. Couldn't know. It's not as if Controllers go around twitching or exchanging Yeerk high fives or playing with their ears. A Controller looks, acts, seems exactly normal.

My father could be my father.

Or he could be screaming, helpless, just beginning to realize that his eyes and ears and mouth no longer belonged to him.

I waited.

And then Tom gave me the clue I was hoping for.

"C'mon, Dad, calm down," he said, going over to him. "We can call and report it when we get home if you want to. Let's go back inside, OK? The meeting just started and a lot of important things are going to happen tonight. You don't want to miss it. Trust me."

"'Go back inside'?" my father echoed, looking at him as if he were insane. "I'm not going back inside! Somebody just tried to break into every car on this street! I'm going home right now and calling Joe Johnson!"

"Who?"

"He's our insurance agent, you really should know that, Tom. Come on."

"But, Dad," Tom pleaded, shooting a furious, agitated look back at Chapman, who stood on the kerb watching them.

The high wail of distant police sirens split the night.

Chapman shook his head slightly.

"I'm staying till the end of the meeting," Tom said sullenly.

"Then I'll expect you home by ten." My father unlocked the car and got in.

Face tight and twisted with ill-concealed rage, Tom stalked over and stood on the kerb next to Chapman, watching as my father drove away.

<He's clean,> I said as an owl landed silently on a nearby ledge. <He's clean. He's OK.>

<Yeah,> Marco said. <Let's get going.>

<Deal,> I said, letting the falcon's keen senses carry me swiftly home.

<Jake? That's round one. You know that,> Marco said, after a moment.

<Yeah,> I said. <I know.>

The fight to save my father had only begun.

Chapter 8

"I can't believe you took that kind of chance," Rachel said, scowling. "You should have waited for the rest of us!"

It was late that night and we'd all sneaked out to meet in Cassie's barn to work out what to do next.

It wasn't going well.

I was distracted, nervous leaving my father alone in the house with Tom.

Tobias was perched high in the rafters.

Marco was strangely quiet.

Cassie was listening, her face filled with distress.

Ax was watching me with all four eyes.

And Rachel. . .

Well, she was just plain mad.

Apparently Erek had got word about our search for my father to Rachel, who'd been shopping at the mall.

She'd rushed to back us up, stowing her packages in a rented locker. In her hurry, she'd forgotten to lock it.

By the time she'd morphed, found Tobias, and flown north, The Sharing meeting had completely closed down. They'd found nothing but cops writing vandalism reports.

When she'd gone back to the locker for her packages, someone had stolen them.

A mad Rachel is a scary thing, and I didn't envy the thief if she ever caught him.

"We weren't looking at a battle, we were just creating a diversion," I said. "Otherwise we'd have waited for you."

I didn't look at Marco as I said it.

<It was an urgent situation,> Ax said calmly.

"Exactly."

Tobias was in the rafters. He ruffled his wings. <A temporary victory. As long as your dad is trying to force Tom to go with you guys, your dad's in danger.>

"I know," I said wearily. "I've thought of trying to convince my dad to lighten up, but there's no way. He's not going to let Tom show disrespect for Grandpa G."

"This is so stupid," Rachel said. "I mean, we're suddenly in a knockdown, drag-out fight

because of some funeral? This is idiotic! This is a nothing fight. No possible gain for us. All we can do is get hammered."

I nodded. "Believe me, I know, Rachel. It's out of nowhere."

"Had to be *four* days," Marco complained. "Couldn't be two days, which would be no biggie to the Yeerk."

<You will not attend this burial ceremony, Rachel?> Ax asked.

"No, I'm not really related," Rachel said. "Grandpa G was Jake's great-grandfather on his mother's side. We're related on his father's side."

<Ah. And that is important?>

<You know, maybe I'm not getting it, but why didn't Tom just tell your father he's not going and that's the end of it?> Tobias interrupted.

I looked at him.

So did the rest of us.

<What?> he asked, sounding defensive. <I used to do that whenever one of my aunts or uncles wanted me to go somewhere I didn't want to. They never made me go.> He was quiet a moment. Then, abashed, he said, <Oh. Duh. They didn't care what I did.>

"Your relatives are jerks and they didn't deserve you," Rachel snapped.

"My father said we're going as a family," I said. "And knowing my father, Tom would stir up more trouble than he could handle by directly defying him, you know?"

"Sure," Marco agreed. "It's hard to get to those Kandrona rays when you're grounded for life."

"Plus, if he acted really badly, then I'm sure your parents would start looking at him differently," Cassie added. "They might even decide The Sharing is a bad influence and try to make him quit."

I nodded. "Tom's Yeerk is passing as a normal, high-school kid. Bottom line, he can either follow family rules or he loses his cover. The Yeerks have a choice: keep Tom in place by infesting my father. Or withdraw Tom's Yeerk, put him into a new host, and kill Tom to keep him from talking."

"There's another choice," Rachel said.

"Yeah," I said. I knew. I just couldn't make myself say it out loud.

"What choice?" Cassie asked.

"If the Yeerks can't make his father into a Controller soon enough, they could just kill him. As an orphan Tom's cover isn't affected. Might even be enhanced," Rachel said. And then, looking me straight in the eye, she said, "And Tom would probably be the one to do it."

Chapter 9

There was only one way to protect my father.

Surveillance.

From the moment he left the house for work in the morning until we left for the cabin on Saturday.

Twenty-four-hour surveillance.

I could do most of it. He was my father and although I didn't say it because I didn't want to hurt anyone's feelings, I really didn't think anybody would watch him as carefully as I would.

I did agree to some back-up. I knew I couldn't be everywhere at once.

The next morning Tom was all sweet reason and compromise. He went out early, claiming he'd talk to some of the kids from The Sharing before school. See if they'd cover for the commitments he'd made.

Right.

I waited until my father was in the shower, then called to excuse myself from school due to a death in the family.

Luckily, I sound enough like my father.

I went down and lurked in the living room outside the kitchen. I heard the sounds of my father getting ready to leave: slurped coffee, the ritual checking of his beeper, the "Ow!" as he burned his fingers getting a muffin out of the toaster.

Stupid to morph in the dining room. Idiotic. But I was going to roach morph and I couldn't travel far on those six little legs. Besides, Tom was gone. And my dad wouldn't come this way.

I focused on the roach.

Not my favourite morph. Not anyone's favourite morph. But I needed to be small, fast and survivable. Maybe a fly would have been better but I'd had a close call as a fly once: someone swatted me and smeared me all over the storage rack on a plane.

Roaches are harder to kill.

I felt the changes begin. So creepy at the best of times. But standing there in my dining room, shrinking as the chairs grew, shrivelling down towards the wooden floor you'd gouged with a rake when you were four, falling into the

shadow of the table where you ate your Thanksgiving meal . . . that added a level of weird.

I caught sight of myself unexpectedly in the dining room sideboard mirror. The skin of my face was turning brown, glossy, hard.

I looked away. You don't want to see yourself turning into a cockroach. You don't want to see the way your mouth divides into insect mouthparts. You don't want to watch your skin melt like wax under a blowtorch and then re-form into a hard, stiff armour. You don't want to be making eye contact with yourself when your eyes stop being eyes and become expressionless black pinheads.

Maybe you'd think we'd all be used to it. Speaking for myself, at least, no. I'll never be used to it.

Morphing may be a great weapon. It is also a horror beyond imagining.

My bones dissolved. There was a liquid, squishing sound.

A pair of twitching, hairy, jointed roach legs exploded from my swollen insect body like a scene out of an *Alien* movie. I was expecting that. They matched what my arms and legs had become.

Long, feathery antennae sprouted from my forehead.

Crisp, glossy wings cupped my back.

My vision was extremely limited. But my antennae made up for some of that loss. You couldn't call what they did hearing or smell, exactly, more like some weird melding of the two. And yet, not like either.

The plan was for me to hitch a ride with my dad. Tobias would be gaining altitude, looking to hitch an elevator ride on a thermal. From high up he'd be able to watch almost all of my dad's drive from home to his office. Three kilometres, give or take.

But his reaction time would necessarily be slow. He'd be back-up, but if there was an attack it'd be up to me.

I was a roach. I turned like a tiny tank and motored beneath the door.

Whoooom. Whoooom.

My dad's footsteps. Vibration and breeze. My antennae fixed his location. I fought down the roach brain's desire to run.

Whoooom. Whooooom.

Feet the size of an aircraft carrier floated past in the dim distance. No problem. I had roach senses and roach speed married to human intelligence. I was safe.

Safe until I got ready to hitch a ride. My dad wore cuffed trousers. The cuff. That would be the place to ride safe and secure.

Just a question of getting there. Up on to the shoe. Up the sock. Should be no problem.

Right.
Light change! Movement! Above me!
I dodged.
BAMMMMM!

Chapter 10

It was the size of one of those big oil storage tanks you see on the outskirts of the city. It was ten times my height. A million times my negligible weight. It hit the linoleum floor like a bomb.

Raspberry jam.

The jar slammed into the ground two centimetres from me.

CRASH! The glass shattered.

Huge globs of jam erupted. A glass shard swathed in goo landed like some kind of meteor beside me. The jam, a wad twice my own size, hit me in the back as I scurried madly away.

My feet scrabbled insanely. Out of control! The roach brain screaming Run! Run! RunRunRun! in my head.

The goo fouled my back legs. I couldn't move!

I fought it, but that just made things worse. I lost my balance and rolled over on to my back, all six legs pushing frantically at the raspberry glue. Seeds like footballs jammed the chinks in my armour.

From far, far up in the stratosphere I heard my dad yell a word he's not supposed to use in front of the kids.

Then I guess he saw me. Because he said a worse word.

And I knew right then: he was going to kill me.

The glass shard! It stuck like a boat prow from the goo. I caught the edge with one leg and pushed. Leverage. Something a roach wouldn't understand. But I did.

A second leg grabbed the glass. It would have sliced human flesh, but my hard twig legs weren't hurt.

I pushed and scrambled, shoved, twisted, fighting my way out of the red goo—

WHAM!

The USS *Nimitz* landed on the floor a millimetre from me as I hauled with all my might.

I was on all sixes again, but the goo was all over me, slowing me, dragging at me as—

WHAM!

The USS *Eisenhower* dropped a millimetre ahead of me.

"——— roach!" a booming voice bellowed. "Now I've got jam all over my shoes!"

You're about to have Jake all over your shoes, I thought. I was getting clear of the jam, but it still clung to my spiky legs. I couldn't get traction. I couldn't get up any speed.

WHAM! The *Eisenhower* again.

The wall of shoe sole, twice my own height, appeared in front of me with horrifying suddenness.

I powered my legs and lunged.

I grabbed the sole. I pulled, I powered, I used all the energy that a combination of roach fear and human terror could provide.

Up! I was on the shoe!

"Where'd it go, the lousy. . ."

I tried to get out of sight. I ran for the shadow of the trouser leg cuff.

"Aaarrrgghh!" he bellowed in a voice that vibrated every molecule of air in the room.

Now came the dancing portion. My father hopped on one foot, the foot I was on, while attempting to crush me with the other foot.

Not happening. Not now. I had my speed back now. I had the curves and swoops of polished leather, the same colour as my own body, to race on.

Running towards the heel, perpendicular to the ground, I hauled. The other shoe poked at me, kicked at me, missed!

At the heel I turned a sharp left and headed vertical. Up the shoe. Over the top on to a soft cotton sock, a sort of grey lawn of scruffy, weirdly twisted grass.

I was in the dark now. Invisible to my father.

"Where'd you go?" he demanded.

Freeze. Just freeze, Jake. Don't move. Don't. . . The jam was very sweet. Very, *very* sweet, and my roach brain craved sweetness. Sugar. The ultimate lure. And it was still on me. On my legs. On my face.

My mouthparts moved.

I could eat the sugar sweetness off my own leg. . .

"Oh! Oh! Oh!" my dad yelled.

He'd felt me. I'd moved. Now I was in trouble.

WHOMPF!

The dark folds of the sky dropped with sickening suddenness as my dad slapped his leg.

WHOMPF!

WHOMPF!

Don't touch the skin! I ordered myself. If I touched the skin he'd know for sure. He wouldn't stop then.

Had to tough it out. Had to hide. Make him think he was wrong, that he hadn't felt me.

The trousers! The grey wool blend that made up the vertical sky. That was the trick.

WHOMPF!

Down it came. I reached, grabbed, and suddenly was lifted away from the sock. I clung to the trousers.

The banging stopped. Slowly the trouser leg was drawn up. But I was in a fold, invisible.

The trouser leg dropped. My dad wiped up the jam and the broken jar, and drove to work.

Chapter 11

The drive was uneventful. I was glad. I couldn't really have taken much more excitement.

Somewhere far above the car Tobias watched. I didn't care. I crept down and out and settled comfortably in the trouser turn-up. I was on the left leg so there wasn't much movement.

Ax was waiting at the parking garage by my dad's building. I could feel the car taking tight turns, going up the ramp.

<I believe I see your father, Prince Jake. Are you with him?>

Ax calls me his prince. It's an Andalite respect thing.

<Yeah, Ax. Barely.>

<You have completed two circuits of the open spiral and have ascended.>

That took a couple of seconds. <Oh. Yeah, it's a ramp. The cars use it to get to higher levels.>

<Yes, Prince Jake, it was not overly difficult for me to deduce the purpose of the open spiral structure,> Ax sniffed.

I'm Ax's "prince". But I suppose the whole respect thing only goes so far.

We parked. I tensed. Things could get hairy again.

The leg swung out into chillier air and brighter light.

My dad stood up. Stretched. Pulled his medical bag out of the backseat. And we were off to the office.

Swing forward. . . Crunch! . . . Swing back. Swing forward. . . Crunch! . . . Swing back.

<Jake, I'm here,> Tobias reported in. <No sign that anyone followed you.>

<That was quick travel!> I said.

<Soon as I saw you guys leave I headed here. And I was already more than half the way here.>

Somewhere above me, invisible to my roach senses, were a red-tailed hawk and, if Ax had followed the plan, a seagull.

<There is a human watching Jake's father closely,> Ax reported. <He is a large human with more than the typical amount of facial fur. He appears to be forming facial expressions associated with anger.>

<An angry bearded guy?> Tobias translated. <Can't see him. Must still be under the. . . OK, I got him. Yeah. He does look angry about something. But he's not making any kind of move.>

My dad stopped walking. Wooosh. A door opening. We moved. Closing behind us.

We were in.

As soon as my father stepped into his own office I shot down his leg and hid under the rubbish bin near his desk.

Waited.

No frantic swiping disturbed the air currents.

Good. Then he hadn't even known I'd hitched a ride.

The floor trembled.

Someone was walking towards my father's office.

"Good morning, Doc. We have a full schedule today. It's ear infection central out there."

Ten minutes later the first kid came in with his mum.

I spent the day zigging and zagging, zipping along the walls and squeezing into crevices to avoid being seen and squashed.

Every two hours I demorphed and remorphed in the toilet. The first time it was nerve-wracking. I scrawled a hasty note on a piece of paper towel and stuck it on to the last cubicle with some used gum.

The note said OUT OF ORDER.

After that I felt a little safer in the out-of-order cubicle.

It was boring beyond belief. But it gave me a lot of time to think. Too much time.

I'd started out hoping this crisis would give me a way to destroy Tom's Yeerk. Now I was down to hoping I could save my dad from Tom's fate.

I was playing a defensive game. It's easier to attack. On the attack you can pick the time and place. On the defence all you can do is wait. Wait for the enemy to pick his time and his place. And wear out your resources and your people waiting, waiting, knowing all it takes is for the enemy to get lucky and all your tense, cramped-up waiting will be for nothing.

My dad's never been my doctor. I go to one of his partners. You know, it'd be creepy otherwise.

I'd always thought it was pretty cool that he was a doctor. But I guess I hadn't really thought much about it.

On this day, though, there wasn't much else to focus on. So I focused on my dad. Always nice. Always gentle. Joking with the kids and reassuring the mums and dads. Staying calm while the littler kids screamed bloody murder and vibrated the very walls.

He was a good guy, my dad. Not just because he was my dad. Because he was a good person.

Because he did his work as well as he knew how and wasn't a jerk to the people around him. That doesn't make you a saint or anything, but I suppose when I think about it, that's what I hope I'll do when I'm older: treat my family right, do my job well, not be a jerk to the people I meet. Maybe that's not a huge, ambitious goal, but it would be enough for me. I've done the hero thing. You can have the hero thing. Me, I wanted a day when all I'd have to do was be a decent human being.

It was a long day.

"Good night, everyone," my dad called, finally. "I'll be back Wednesday at the latest. Have a good weekend, Jeannie. You, too, Mary Anne. Stay out of trouble."

A laugh followed us out of the door. Now we were moving.

My father was heading out of the office. Back into possible danger.

<OK, guys, we're moving towards you. We'll be back in the car park in a couple of minutes,> I called.

<Hey, Jake?> Tobias said worriedly. <Uh, I don't know if this means anything but the bearded guy is back, hanging around near the lift.>

<Which floor?> I asked, although I already knew.

The one my father was parked on, of course.

Tobias confirmed it. Ax confirmed it, too.

Hesitate at the door. Then we were outside.

My antennae quivered at the change in the air.

No time to demorph and remorph. If the bearded guy was part of an attack, I was useless.

Nothing but a roach in a turn-up.

<Ax?>

<Yes,> Ax said. <I am by your father's vehicle.>

<Is there any place you can morph without being seen?> I asked.

<I have been demorphing behind a large rubbish receptacle in the alley behind this structure; however, I cannot get back from there to my present position without being seen,> Ax replied. <Should I proceed?>

I didn't know.

If an Andalite suddenly arrived on the scene to save my father, the Yeerks would put two and two together, realize someone close to Tom — like his little brother — knew about his plan, and the Animorphs would be dead.

But in our present morphs, we'd be helpless.

What should I do?

Lose everyone?

Or just my father?

Chapter 12

<Prince Jake, do you have any instructions for me?>

<Jake. Make the call, man.>

My family or my friends.

Save one man or save the world.

I was a bug! I couldn't save anyone.

An overt rescue would save my dad and doom us all. Including him.

<What's happening now?> I asked.

<Your father is walking towards his car,> Ax said. <The man with the facial fur is following him.>

<How close?>

<He's about a metre and a half behind your dad,> Tobias said. He was tense. <And closing fast.>

I scampered up and out of the turn-up. On to the trouser leg. Around to the back of the knee. The fabric crinkled with each step. I was horizontal, with the ground on my right. I couldn't see far enough to be sure, but there seemed to be a large, dark wall moving in behind my father. <Am I looking at him?>

<Yes,> Ax said.

OK. Fine. I might be in a bug's body but I still had a human brain.

I hauled a left and went vertical. Up the trousers. On to the jacket. Up the jacket. Zooming at roach speed along a vertical plane of dry wool fibres.

I came to a stop on the slope of a shoulder. An ear the size of a container truck loomed above me.

Closer. The dark wall was coming closer. I could almost see a face, a blur, a bristling mass bigger than a rain cloud.

<Jake, what're you doing?> Tobias asked sharply.

<I'm doing what a roach does best,> I said.

<What?>

<Grossing people out and making them say. . .>

I motored. I cranked open the roach's almost useless wings. I flew straight for that beard.

"Aaaahhhhh!" the man yelled.

I landed on his lower lip. The tiny hairs on my legs caught and clung.

He spat. A hurricane explosion of wind!

But I was down on his chin hairs now, walking gingerly from split hair to split hair, like I was tiptoeing across treetops.

"Ugh! Ugh! A beetle!" the man shouted. We began to spin and whirl. He slapped his own face. "Get it off me!"

I zigged left. Then right.

Motored towards his ear. Little roach feet tickled waxy ear skin.

He went wild.

I kept going, on up to his head. On to thick, matted hair.

"What the heck. . ." I heard my father say in astonishment. "Excuse me, sir, but are you all right?"

Go! I wanted to tell him. *Run, Dad! Run for your life!*

<On our way, Jake!> Tobias yelled.

<NO!> I yelled. <Back off! Back off!>

Suddenly, the air rushed and shimmered with the swoosh of wings.

"Tseeeeeer!" Tobias swooped down, talons extended. I caught an indistinct but terrifying flash of ripping talons.

"Aaaahhh! Aaaahhh!" the man yelled. He was literally beating at his face with one hand to kill me and waving the other in the air to fight off the lunatic hawk and the insane seagull.

Quite suddenly I realized I was no longer on the man. I was on his hair. But I was not on the man any more.

The hair . . . the toupee . . . was in Tobias's talons being carried off like a doomed mouse.

<I'm going to circle back for—> Tobias began.

<No! No!> I yelled, angry. <We might as well tattoo "The Animorphs were here" on the guy's head! Stay back. Don't attack unless you see the beard move to attack.>

<Oh. Yeah.>

<This is not an attack,> Ax said. <Your father and the man with the facial fur are making mouth-sounds. If this were a Yeerk attack they would not be making mouth-sounds together.>

<Drop the rug,> I instructed Tobias.

He did. The toupee hit the concrete and the man snatched it up and slapped it back on his head. I dropped out before he did and, with Tobias's help, headed in the direction of my dad.

"The bird's gone, the roach is gone, you're OK," my father said soothingly.

"Forget the stupid bug! Forget the stupid, stupid bird!" the man yelled.

He was clearly upset. A hawk had seemingly attempted to grab a cockroach off his head and

ended up flying off with his toupee. That's the kind of thing that will put you in a bad mood.

"Is that your car?" the bald man demanded.

"Huh?"

"I said, IS THAT YOUR CAR?!" the man roared.

Like I said, upset.

"Yes," my father said, sounding puzzled. "Why?"

"Because it's parked in *my* spot! MY spot! Mine! I've been waiting to see who keeps taking my spot!"

"How can this be your spot?" my father asked. "There aren't any spots marked 'reserved' here."

"I've been parking in this spot for two years and four months! It's my spot! I don't care how many birds or . . . or my toupee . . . or bugs . . . it's mine!"

<I do not believe this man is a Controller,> Ax said.

<What was your *first* clue, Ax-man?> Tobias said.

<My first clue is the fact that this human is not—>

<It was a rhetorical question,> Tobias said.

<Ah.>

No attack. An argument over a parking space. Funny, really.

Except that I was still left fighting the losing, defensive battle.

Worse, I had frozen. Tobias and Ax had asked for orders and I had frozen. Because I had frozen they'd made the wrong move.

My fault, not theirs. I was in charge, they'd asked me what to do.

I'd hesitated. I'd had no answer. No harm, this time. But if the attack had been real?

I was tired. Ax and Tobias were tired. We were measurably diminished, and the enemy had lost nothing.

The attack was still to come.

Chapter 13

I cut Tobias and Ax loose. Told them to get some rest. Tobias objected. He said he'd get the others, they'd mount a surveillance on my house.

I blew him off. Told him to let everyone rest.

Why? I don't know. Maybe I wanted to handle it myself. That way there would be no orders to give. And no second-guessing.

My dad pulled into the garage and I scampered away. I demorphed behind the garage and raced up to my room.

I beat my dad inside. See, I knew his routine. When he comes home he walks down to our letterbox at the kerb to check the post and stands there going through it muttering, "Junk . . . junk . . . OK, magazine . . . junk."

I was in my bed in seconds. Covers up to my chin. Playing sick.

"Jake?"

My door opened. Tom stuck his head into the room.

"What?" I croaked, having a heart failure. I hadn't realized he was home. Had he been home while I'd been demorphing? "When did you get home?"

"What are you doing? Faking sick?"

The Yeerk in his head played the role. Said the words Tom would have said.

I played my role, too. "Yeah. Wanted to stay home and watch Jerry Springer."

"Uh-huh."

"I'm feeling better now, though. I think I'll get up."

He gave me a disgusted look and left. I climbed out of bed and got dressed.

Dinner was chicken soup for me. To "soothe" my upset stomach. My father and brother wolfed down Chinese food.

"What time are we leaving tomorrow?" I asked.

"About nine, so you boys pack tonight and don't forget your suits," my father said, missing Tom's sudden, black scowl. "I talked to your mum. The funeral's on Monday and we'll be leaving for home Tuesday morning."

Tom shoved back his chair. "I'm done," he said, rising and stalking off.

My dad studiously ignored him. "Well, I'm going out to water the lawn one last time before we leave."

"I'll load the dishwasher," I offered, rising.

I rinsed the plates, watching through the window as my father dragged the hose from the back garden to the front.

The house was so quiet. The air so still.

Tom had disappeared into his room.

I pressed my face to the window, leaving a nose smear, and searched the sky until I spotted Tobias gliding high above.

Keeping watch, though I hadn't asked him to.

He looked so free out there.

So calm and confident.

I straightened. Looked around.

And made my decision.

Five minutes, I thought, hurrying up to my room and locking the door behind me. I'll do a five-minute, aerial surveillance. Just enough flying to get hold of myself again. Reassure myself. I'm no good to anybody if I can't think straight.

I stripped down to my cycling shorts, opened the window, and concentrated on my peregrine falcon morph.

A lacy pattern rose and spread across my skin, softening into feathers. My fingers melted together to form wing tips as my guts gurgled, slithered, and shifted.

My skull ground and shrunk. My vision sharpened. I zoomed downwards, falling, shrinking, wobbling on suddenly skinny, stick legs.

The breeze drifted in the window.

I flapped my wings and hopped up to the sill. Weird. After all this time the idea of jumping out of the first-floor window still bothered me. I was still human, still scared of heights, still not sure my wings would work. I wondered if Tobias ever felt that way.

I spread my wings and took off, swooping down across the back garden, taking care to stay away from Tom's bedroom window.

I caught a slight headwind, just enough to fill my wings, and began to work for altitude.

<Is that you, Jake?> Tobias called cautiously.

<Yeah, I decided I'd join you for a couple of minutes,> I said, levelling off and drifting along on an air current. My falcon eyes could see everything, including a mouse scurrying along the neighbour's fence.

And my dad watering the lawn.

<How's it going?> I asked Tobias.

<I'm getting very little lift in this air,> he complained.

I smiled to myself. A typical Tobias answer.

<How's it going with you?> he asked.

<Tense,> I admitted. <It's very tense down there. My dad, Tom, armed camps, man. And me in the middle.>

Tobias didn't say anything. I looked at him. He was higher than me, maybe two hundred metres off.

<Tobias?>

No answer.

<Tobias! What's—>

<Chapman! It *is* him. I couldn't be sure in this light. Six blocks from your house. Him driving, some other guy in the passenger seat.>

I followed the direction of his gaze. A dark car, large, four-door. I focused my gaze. Was the passenger holding something?

<I don't like the feel of this,> I said.

<No,> Tobias agreed.

<My dad—>

<Gun!> Tobias yelled. <The passenger. He's got a gun!>

Chapter 14

I was in a dive before Tobias had finished the sentence.

They were going to pull a drive-by. It was insane. A shooting in broad daylight? Just how important was Tom to the Yeerks? This was reckless!

I was falling . . . no, not falling. I was a rocket on a collision course with Earth. Aimed like a cruise missile for my own house.

The car turned one street closer to mine.

I flared my wings to brake. The hurricane of wind nearly broke them. I strained every muscle, spread every feather. I landed, skidding on the back side of the roof.

No time to demorph inside.

I'd just have to take my chances out here,

tucked into the shadowy corner. I began to demorph.

<Jake, what are you doing?> Tobias cried.

I could have answered. I didn't. Tobias knew what I was doing.

<This is stupid, Jake, but I'll cover your butt anyway,> Tobias said. <Don't see anyone watching you. Possible line of sight to the house behind and to the left. There's a little girl near her window.>

My feathers melted. My arms fattened. My beak softened like it was melting. I had to scramble to hold on with talons that were becoming stubby human toes.

<Here comes Chapman,> Tobias reported grimly.

NO!

Demorph! Demorph! Demorph!

Toes . . . hands . . . face. . .

"Aaahhh!" I yelled in surprise.

Suddenly, I was sliding down the steep roof towards the edge.

<Jake! Your brother's right there in the kitchen on the phone!> Tobias shouted. <If you come down on that side, he's going to see you!>

My fingers scrabbled across the rough shingles for a handhold but it was no use. My fingernails were practically liquid.

I was falling.

Over the edge!

Desperate, I grabbed the sharp, metal gutter.

Dangled. Arms stretched. I tried to haul my legs up, out of view.

<Tom hasn't seen you yet,> Tobias said. <He's got his back to the window. But Chapman is twenty seconds away. It's now or never.>

Tom's voice drifted out through the window.

"Perfect timing," he said coldly. "He's out front alone. Go for it."

I dropped, hit the grass with a dull thud, and gritted my teeth to stay quiet. I crawled past the window, then shot to my feet and tore round the house.

A dark car was turning on to my block. A hundred metres away. Fifty.

"Hey, Dad." I limped over to him, sweating, heart thundering. "Let me do that."

I took the hose.

My dad smiled. "Volunteering, huh? So. What is it you want?"

Twenty metres!

"Just wanted to get outside. Fresh air," I said.

"Unh. Well, thanks, then. I'll go do some packing."

He turned. Too slowly! He walked. Too slowly!

The car was there.

The window was down.

The gunman was staring at my father's back.

I jerked the hose. Water hit the side of the car.

The gunman yanked back in surprise; my father opened the door.

I waved at the car and said, "Sorry!"

The car passed by.

I breathed. My hands were shaking. My heart was a jackhammer.

I pretended to suddenly recognize Mr Chapman as the car pulled away. "Hey, Mr Chapman!" I waved.

I felt someone watching me. I spared a quick glance. Tom.

He was framed in our living room window. His eyes burned with rage.

He'd have killed me, too. He would have had my dad gunned down and if I'd got in the way. . .

And that wasn't the worst of it. Worse was knowing that my brother Tom, my true brother, had been trapped inside his own mind, trapped watching as the killers prepared to murder his family. Helpless, watching, unable to open his own mouth to shout a warning.

I was clenching the hose so tightly the water was petering out. But I couldn't relax the muscles. Could not.

I don't know how this war will turn out. Don't know if we'll win or lose or even, somehow, compromise and make peace. But I know one thing: I will kill the Yeerk who has done this to my brother.

I will kill him.

Chapter 15

We met in Cassie's barn. All of us but Ax and Rachel. They were watching my house. My dad would be safe with those two.

Tobias calmly, without blame, related what had happened that day and afternoon.

"Stupid," Marco said.

"I can't believe you took a chance like that, Jake!" Cassie said angrily. Cassie doesn't get mad, but she was mad. "Were you *looking* to get shot?!"

"Obviously not," I said, meeting her gaze. "But what else was I supposed to do? Let them kill my father?"

"That's not the point," Marco said, as angry as Cassie, but colder about it. "You demorphed in plain view. And Tobias says it was a matter of a split second whether you ended up machine-gunned on your own lawn."

"The alternative was letting them gun down my father."

"So you decided to let them kill you, too?"

"It worked!" I raged.

Marco threw up his hands in disgust. "Why didn't you have back-up? Tobias says you told him and Ax to get lost. And not to get any of us," Marco said. He was leaning back on a bale of hay. Leaning back, but not at all relaxed. "We're supposed to be in this together. If you needed help, you were supposed to ask for it."

"Yeah, I know," I said. "But you guys were in school during the surveillance and tonight, well, I didn't exactly expect Chapman to do a drive-by shooting, you know."

"A mistake on your part," Marco said.

"Yeah. A mistake."

"And today, earlier? Tobias says you froze up when he asked for an order."

"I didn't freeze up, I—"

"We can't afford you freezing up," Marco said.

I glared at him. "You're enjoying this, aren't you? This is payback for when I doubted you over your mother."

"I was ready to do what had to be done," Marco said.

"So am I!"

"No. You're not. You endangered all of us. You demorphed on your roof! On your roof! In daylight. With your brother in the house! If Tom had seen you do that you'd be head down in the Yeerk pool right now, and the rest of us would be standing in line behind you!"

"What's the matter with you all?!" I cried. "That was my father! My father! I'm supposed to just stand by and do nothing?"

Tobias answered before Marco could. <Is it worth exposing ourselves and risking everything, all of mankind . . . literally all the human race . . . just to save one person?> he said quietly. <I'm sorry, Jake. I know he's your father. I know what you're feeling. But it's something we have to think about.>

I looked away. My face was burning. "You know, we talked about this and we decided on surveillance. We watched my father in case he needed protection. Well, he did and I reacted. What did you guys really think I was going to do?"

"Just what you did," Marco said. "You're too close to this. You can't make this call."

I barked out a laugh. "What, you're going to decide whether my dad lives or dies?" I looked at Cassie.

"Jake. . ." she said.

"You need to back off on this," Marco said quietly. "You can't make this call. Not about your dad and your brother."

"You made it when it was your mum," I said.

Marco shrugged. "Yeah, well, that's me. If it's any comfort to you, I'd like myself more if I was like you. But the question here is, how far do we go to protect your father?" Marco said. "And who is going to make that decision?"

"I'm the leader of this group," I said.

Marco hesitated. He bit his lip. Then, drawing a deep breath, he said, "We need a vote."

"Rachel and Ax aren't here," I said.

<Ax will refuse to vote,> Tobias said. <He'll say it's a human question. He'll say Jake is his prince and he'll do what his prince says. But he won't cast a vote either way.>

"Rachel will back me," I said.

Marco nodded. "Yeah. She will. That leaves it up to Cassie and Tobias."

I didn't look at either of them. I expected to hear Cassie speak up. But she didn't. Silence.

I felt like the ground was falling away beneath me. Cassie doubted me, too? Cassie didn't think I could handle this?

I heard a ruffling of feathers up in the rafters and looked up. Tobias cocked his head, his fierce hawk's gaze meeting my angry, human one.

I was the first to look away.

Tobias had been there twice when I'd risked my life — and his — to save my father. He knew

how important it was to me and he knew how far I'd go to do it.

<You guys are missing a couple of important points,> Tobias said quietly. <First of all, writing off a human life is something the Yeerks would do, not us.>

Cassie nodded. She looked troubled. Like she should have thought of that.

<Second, what if the Yeerks don't *kill* Jake's father? What if they succeed instead in making him a Controller?> Tobias continued. <Jake's already got one Controller in his family; if they make his father one, too, then there's going to be a couple of very suspicious people watching Jake coming and going all the time, especially when there's Animorph activity. So I don't think it's a question of *should* we save him, but how we do it.>

Thank you, Tobias, I thought silently, staring down at the ground.

<But there's one more thing that nobody's talking about,> Tobias continued, stretching and refolding his wings. <I think we've been on the wrong path all this time. Sitting around waiting for the Yeerks to attack, then saving Jake's father again and again is no plan. The Yeerks may think it was a coincidence at the mall, maybe a coincidence on the lawn, but they can count, you know? Sooner or later they'll think, "That's too many coincidences.">

"Exactly," Marco said.

<So, why don't we get off the defensive? Do something. Something big that'll distract their attention away from Jake's father until he and Tom and Jake can leave for the cabin tomorrow morning?>

Marco hesitated. He knew the vote had gone against him. At worst he had Cassie on his side. That was two against three, leaving Ax out.

Finally Marco nodded. "OK, we go on the offensive." He tried a semblance of his usual humour. "I always wanted to die kicking and screaming."

He stepped towards me. He held out his hand. "Nothing personal, Jake. I was just looking out for the group."

I left his hand hanging in mid-air.

After a while he withdrew it.

"So, what's the plan?" Cassie said, trying to break the hostility of that moment.

"Maybe we could think about—" Marco began.

"I have a plan," I said.

Chapter 16

Did I have a plan? Not till that split second. Not till I was face-to-face with Marco and realizing I had to come up with something. Had to.

Sometimes emotion works for you.

We needed a distraction. The distraction I had in mind was big. And would hopefully last until I could get my father out of town.

"Kidnap Chapman," I said.

That made Marco stare. It drew a gasp from Cassie. Tobias laughed like I might be joking. Then he sort of moaned.

Then he laughed again and said, <Well, I'll say one thing: this is going to make Rachel happy.>

A daring plan? Yes.

Crazy? Suicidal? Stupid?

I hoped not.

"Forces the Yeerks to decide their priorities," Marco said. "Do they save Tom or Chapman? Who's more important to them? Chapman. They'll still try and help Tom with his situation, but Chapman disappearing will be a total Alert, Maximum Panic situation. It works."

Give Marco credit for one thing: no one is faster or better at seeing the ruthless solution. And Marco is honest.

It wasn't going to be a pretty mission. We didn't have time for subtle.

We hooked up with Rachel and Ax and explained the plan.

Rachel said, "Cool!"

I left Cassie and Tobias to guard my house. I'd have left Marco, too, but he would have taken it as me being afraid to have him around. I wasn't going to give him the satisfaction.

Rachel, Ax, Marco and I flew to a house across the street and down from Chapman's home on a quiet, suburban street. It was dark. Not late, but dark. I was twenty minutes away from my dad wondering why I wasn't home. Same with the others.

The house was for sale. Vacant. The bushes were overgrown and untended. Perfect for us. Almost roomy at first. Less so as we morphed.

"Move over, Marco," Rachel grumbled as his shoulders bulged and muscled up into a gorilla's massive form.

"Oh, come on, you love being close to me," he leered, just before his jaw swung out and his lips became a puffy, black rubber Halloween mask.

I shut my eyes and concentrated on my own morph.

Rhinoceros. For this job we needed blunt, brute force. And nothing is blunter than a rhino.

I heard the thin bone of my human skull crunch and split apart. Heard a sound like grinding teeth as new bone, layers and layers of new bone, filled in the gaps and made an almost impenetrable armour.

My body thickened. My legs, arms, hands, feet, stomach, back, shoulders, all thickened. My skin thickened from human flesh to something resembling a car's leather seat to something as tough and dense and stiff as a saddle.

My ears crawled up the sides of my head.

My eyesight dimmed and blurred.

My neck lost all definition, sucking back into my expanding, blimplike body. Bigger. Bigger.

Huge.

And then, at last, the horn. It grew from my face, down where my nose had once been. Long, curved, dangerous. A primitive, blunt weapon. A horn that could have impaled an armoured knight.

But despite the formidable body, the terrifying horn, the power of the rhino, its mind was peaceful, placid. Basically, it just wanted to eat and to be left alone. It was watchful but not scared or angry.

That was OK. I had enough fear and anger for both of us.

"Prince Jake, I am ready. Red-eeee. Eeeee," Ax said. He'd morphed to human, using the DNA combination he'd long ago absorbed from all of us. But he'd stopped the morph partway, distorting his features so Chapman wouldn't be able to recognize him later on.

In his standard human morph, Ax is a strange and beautiful kid. Now, with his eyes a little beadier, his nose stubby and squashed, and his hair darker and shaggier, he bore a startling resemblance to Quasimodo.

Minus the hump, of course.

<Well, Ax, I'll never again think of you as just another pretty face,> Marco said.

<Do you guys see anything suspicious?> I interrupted, twisting my ears around at each new sound and sniffing the air. <I'm half blind with these eyes.>

<Suspicious? Well, I see a bear, a gorilla, a rhino and some weird kid standing in the bushes, but aside from that, no,> Marco said.

I didn't laugh. I didn't find Marco funny right then. I missed Tobias. We had no one in the air, and we had to cross the street.

<Come on, let's do this,> Rachel said impatiently.

<Ax, move out,> I ordered. <Marco, you, too.>

Ax began to cross the street. It was quiet. I heard bare human feet and bare gorilla feet. I saw shapes, shadows, little else. But I had excellent hearing. I did not hear any approaching cars.

Marco walked as much like a human as he could. A two-hundred-kilo human. Once across the street he sidled into the bushes beside the porch. Ax walked up Chapman's porch and knocked on the door.

A wait of several seconds.

The door swung open.

Chapman stood there, holding a newspaper and looking irritated at being interrupted.

"Hello, is Melissa here? Hee-yer? I am a friend of Melissa? I have come here to speak to her regarding a class assignment. Class-uh," Ax said brightly, more or less following the script we'd worked out.

Chapman peered out at Ax and frowned. Sighed. "Wait here. I'll get her."

"Good," Ax said. "She is my close friend and also classmate and thus this is a perfectly normal thing for me to do."

Chapman gave him another look and went to get her.

<Ax,> I whispered. <What do you see?>

<It is as you suspected, Prince Jake,> Ax said. <This Controller has added security devices since

our last infiltration. There are motion sensors camouflaged as a mirror frame in the front hallway. And I suspect Dracon beams concealed in the eyes of a statuette facing the doorway.>

<OK then,> I said as my adrenalin started pumping. <Everyone be ready.>

<I've been ready,> Rachel said grimly.

The front door opened and Melissa stepped out. The door closed behind her.

She looked puzzledly at Ax.

Before she could say anything, two thick, hairy gorilla arms reached up over the railing and lifted her off the steps and down into the bushes.

"Aaahh!" she yelped before a massive hand clapped over her mouth.

Melissa was an innocent. She didn't need to see what was going to happen next.

<Got her tied up!> Marco yelled.

<Go! Go! Go!> I yelled.

Chapter 17

<Go! Go! Go!>

I burst from the bushes. Rachel was right beside me, moving in the deceptively fast, rolling gait of the grizzly bear.

Ax leaped from the porch and rolled under cover to demorph.

I crossed the untended lawn, focusing my dim sight on the porch light across the street. But as my massive head swung left and right I lost sight of it. Lights. Everywhere! Which was. . .

<Jake! You're drifting left!> Marco yelled.

I veered. Across the hard concrete of the street. A car! Twin lights raced towards me from my left.

Screeeeeeech!

The driver slammed the brakes. I ignored him. Too late to worry. *Smash and grab and forget subtlety*, I reminded myself.

I stumbled as my thick, tree-trunk legs connected with the porch steps.

<That's it!> Marco yelled.

I barrelled, full speed, heedless, horn down for the door.

WHAM-CRUNCH!

The door exploded inward. The frame ripped. Plaster and moulding showered.

"HHROOO-UH!" Rachel bellowed, right behind me.

TSEEEEW! TSEEEEW!

Hot, screaming pain. The stench of sizzling hair and flesh.

The Dracon beam in the statuette fired again, burning another black, smoking hole in my armoured hide.

It hurt just enough to make me even madder. Now the rhino brain was enraged, too.

I drove forward, through the doorway, slammed into the far wall and knocked the Dracon-concealing statuette over.

Crash!

TSEEEW!

It fired one last, scorching, agonizing beam up into my belly before I crushed it beneath my feet.

Mrs Chapman ran out from the kitchen.

"Andalites!" she yelled and levelled a handheld Dracon beam right at my face.

TSEEEEEW!

Searing heat sizzled my forehead, my ear, drilled a burning hole into my very brain, and I staggered, bellowing as the sledgehammer pain rocked me.

The rhino was hurt. Badly.

"GRRROOOWWRRR!" Rachel roared. With a paw the size of a man's head she smacked Mrs Chapman and sent her flying into the wall. The woman hit, groaned, and slid to the ground, out of the fight.

A flash of blue fur and Ax was with us. <Chapman is escaping up the stairs!>

<Let him go,> I snapped. <We'll even give him a minute to sound the alarm.>

I was reeling. The rhino had taken a head shot. It was dying. The connections between brain and body were fraying.

I counted to ten. <Long enough. Let's go!>

<He's coming out the back window, upstairs,> Marco reported from outside.

<Ax, up the stairs. Rachel, with me.> I crashed towards the living room. The doorway was too narrow. I widened it.

I trampled over the couch and crushed the coffee table like it was made out of toothpicks.

Through the living room. Through the French windows. Literally *through*.

Chapman dropped from down to my right. Marco was there. Reached for Chapman with—

BLAM! BLAM! BLAM!

Chapman fired a handgun. Primitive human technology. Point-blank.

Marco dropped straight back. He hit the ground. Chapman jumped over him.

<Marco!> Rachel yelled.

An Andalite form soared over my head and landed heavily on the grass. Ax had jumped from the first-floor window.

<Rachel, take care of Marco!> I ordered. <Ax! With me!>

Chapman was climbing his back fence. I hit the wood slats and sent him flying. He rolled on to his back and fired.

BLAM! BLAM!

Hammer blows that connected with my throat.

I staggered, ploughed into Ax, and knocked him off his feet.

Chapman was up and running through the busted fence.

I was hurt, bleeding, reeling, clinging to consciousness.

And clinging, most of all, to rage. This creep had tried to gun down my father.

I hit him.

He flew, hit the ground, and rolled, groaning. The gun was a metre and a half away.

I backed up a step. Tossed my head. Scented the air and targeted his moaning, prone form.

Die, Yeerk.

I charged.

<No, Jake!> Rachel yelled. <We need him alive! Ax! Stop him!>

I was going to scrape Chapman across the ground. Stomp him, crush him, dig my horn into him.

I saw the horror in his eyes as he realized what I meant to do.

<Prince Jake!> Ax yelled.

I charged. Then, at last, the injuries were too much. As if someone had sliced my legs off, I fell. My momentum carried me, skidding into Chapman.

Chapman tried to rise. Ax nailed him with the side of his tail blade. Chapman went down, unconscious.

I was swirling, swirling down into a black pit. Had to demorph. Demorph. It was dark . . . dark enough that Marco couldn't say. . .

Marco. Had I got him killed?

Melissa must have worked the gag out of her mouth. "Mummy? Daddy, where are you?!" Melissa Chapman wailed.

Chapter 18

I demorphed to the sound of Melissa's terrified cries and the wail of approaching police sirens.

I stood up, frazzled, confused. Rachel was there, human. Ax was gone. Marco. . .

Marco reached down and lifted Chapman easily up on to his shoulder.

"You OK?" I asked him.

<Demorphed, remorphed, good as new,> he said tersely. <Let's move out. With your permission, mighty leader.>

We moved. Rachel and me providing what limited visual cover we could for Marco. We ran across the street and down. Back to the vacant "For Sale" house.

We were going to keep Chapman a prisoner right where no one would ever suspect: within

two hundred metres of his own home.

Ax had disconnected the burglar alarm when we got there. The back door was open.

We hustled inside. Marco dropped Chapman unceremoniously in the empty, wood-floored living room. Then he popped his fist through the glass of a door connecting dining room and living room. The glass fell towards Chapman.

With his weak but nimble Andalite fingers Ax tied a rag over Chapman's eyes. Ropes went around his wrists and ankles.

We stood there, looking down at him. He was in our power. For now.

"I wonder—" Rachel started to say.

I shook my head and put my finger to my lips. He couldn't be allowed to hear human voices.

<He is still unconscious,> Ax said.

Marco reached down and poked Chapman in the ribs with a finger like a salami. The Controller did not react.

I went to the kitchen. I found an empty coffee tin someone had used to store nuts and bolts. I filled it with cold water, returned to the living room, and poured it on Chapman's face.

He sputtered and cursed.

Then he tried to move his hands.

<OK, Ax, it's all yours,> Marco said, stepping back.

Rachel and I remained silent.

Ax moved forward, hooves clopping on the bare, wooden floors, circling Chapman on purpose, letting him hear that his interrogator was an Andalite.

<So, Yeerk,> he sneered imperiously. <Now you are mine.>

Chapman started to tremble.

He whimpered, soft and low.

I didn't look at Rachel; she didn't look at me. Neither of us was thrilled about this. We had to make Chapman think he was being interrogated by an Andalite warrior.

We had to make him think he would be tortured. Moments earlier I would have killed him. Even now, I felt no pity for him. But that didn't change the fact that we were trying to terrify another living, sentient creature.

If you're the kind of person who gets off on that, you need help. I was asking a lot of Ax. Too much.

But he was determined to play the role.

<If you want to live — and I need not remind you that it is in my power to end your life right now — you will answer my questions,> Ax said with exaggerated Andalite arrogance. <What is the extent of the Yeerk penetration of Earth?>

Chapman shuddered but stayed silent.

<Do not defy me, Yeerk filth!> Ax roared. <Name all the Yeerks in positions of power!!>

No answer.

<I will keep you here, you know,> Ax said, changing tactics and using a silken, deadly thought-speak voice. <Kandrona starvation, Yeerk. It is a terrible way to die. How long since you visited the Yeerk pool? How many days, how many hours do you have before the terrible need begins to—>

I'd seen and heard enough. I jerked my head towards the door. Rachel and Marco followed me. Marco demorphed as he went.

Ax's words had conjured up a dark, miserable picture in my mind.

The death he had falsely promised Chapman was the one my brother Tom was going to suffer, because the Yeerk in his head would be cut off from Kandrona rays.

"Jake?" Rachel whispered, once we were outside.

I shook my head. Couldn't answer.

I headed for home past the crowd of neighbours and cops and emergency vehicles that had clustered around the Chapman home.

So far, the plan had worked.

Ax would continue to interrogate Chapman.

Maybe get rough with him.

This was what I'd led us to. Marco nearly killed. Melissa Chapman terrorized. And Ax left to spin tales of horror for a helpless captive.

Marco wouldn't need to take another vote: I was done being the leader.

Chapter 19

I lay awake all night.

Tense.

Listening.

Listening to the sounds coming out of the darkness.

Waiting for Tobias, who had settled down two hours ago in the tree outside my window, to suddenly shout, <The Yeerks are coming, Jake!>

It didn't happen.

At 3:30, I slid out of bed, careful not to step on the creaky part of the floor, and tiptoed into the hallway.

My father's door was half-closed.

I peeked in.

He was sleeping, the moonlight shining on his face.

I inched further down the hall.

Tom's door was closed.

I held my breath and pressed my ear to the door.

Nothing.

Palms sweating, I gripped the knob and without wiggling it, slooooowly cracked open the door.

Tom's bed was empty.

I shivered.

Closed the door and hurried back to my own room.

My brother was gone.

Probably out with the rest of the Controllers, searching frantically for Chapman. Tobias must have seen him go but didn't want to wake me up.

I climbed back into bed and lay there, wide-eyed and listening to the house settling.

Wondering what my brother was doing. How he was feeling.

And imagining how frantically the Yeerks were searching for Chapman.

How scared and desperate Tom's Yeerk must be by now, knowing he was suddenly just priority number two.

"Are you scared, Yeerk?" I whispered into the darkness.

I thought about how I'd feel if my friends left me to the Yeerks to save someone more important.

Not a good feeling.

And what about the real Tom inside?

What was he thinking?

I didn't know and I couldn't stand the thought, but I couldn't stop thinking about it.

Couldn't let it go.

I was the leader.

I should have been able to come up with a better, surer plan.

If I couldn't figure out a way to save my own family, then how could the other Animorphs rely on me, anyway?

How could I rely on myself?

My numb, foggy brain begged for sleep but it wasn't happening.

The hours crept by.

<Hey, Jake, are you up? Are you awake? If not, wake up. Your brother just sneaked in through the back door,> Tobias said as the sun rose and my bedroom was filled with brilliant, golden sunlight.

I couldn't answer. Wasn't anything to say anyway.

I heard Tom creep past my room. Heard him open, then close his bedroom door.

I swung wearily out of bed and opened my window.

Time to go check on Chapman.

Chapter 20

I used my peregrine falcon morph and flew to the empty house where Chapman was being held hostage.

I was tempted to continue holding Chapman and starve his Yeerk to death. Let the Yeerk Empire know that they were vulnerable, too. That we could be cruel enough to kill, when pushed far enough.

The sick, dark anger inside me wanted to. And had nearly tried, last night in rhino morph.

I landed in a tree near the window.

Ax was still inside.

<Everything going OK, Ax?> I asked from outside the house.

<Yes, Prince Jake,> Ax replied. <I was careful to walk directly over the glass from the

broken window, making it crunch very loudly. I believe this Controller will use the glass to sever his bonds once I have left.>

<Good,> I said.

<No, Prince Jake, nothing about this is good,> Ax snapped. <This is not behaviour suitable to a warrior. I will not do this again.>

<Understood, Ax,> I said.

<The human daughter of this Controller has walked through the neighbourhood crying for her father. I have heard her. As I have heard the terror of this Controller. I will gladly fight this Controller and even, in fair battle, kill him, but I am not a torturer.>

I'd never heard Ax this mad. Never even close.

<It's my fault, Ax. My responsibility. You only did what I asked you to do, as your prince. This is on me.>

<No. My actions are my actions and are my responsibility,> he said, but his anger had softened a little. <I am sorry to have expressed anger.>

<Ax-man, you are entitled,> I said wearily.

He didn't say anything for a while, and I sat, miserable and ashamed, in the tree.

<I must play out the charade,> Ax said wearily.

<Yeah.>

I sat there, fluffing my feathers against the morning chill, watching as the first early commuters headed for their cars, slung their briefcases and laptops in the backseat, and headed off for work. Normal. A normal day in a normal American suburb.

Except that across the street a girl cried for a father she'd long ago lost without knowing it, and here, a creature part man and part Yeerk was threatened with painful death.

<Kandrona starvation, Yeerk. That is what awaits you. The slow weakening . . . the growing madness . . . the terror as you begin to realize that nothing, nothing can save you. Is that what you want? Help me, Yeerk. Help me help you.> Ax could have used private thought-speak, thought-speak only Chapman would hear. But he wanted me to hear.

<Your last chance. I will leave you here, bound, helpless, the thirst and hunger of your human host body adding to your own desperate need.>

If Chapman answered I didn't hear him. I guess he did answer, though, because Ax said, <Your choice, Yeerk.>

Moments later Ax was morphed to osprey and soaring away from the house.

Chapman would escape. We had left the broken glass there deliberately. Chapman believed we were all Andalites. He would think we were too unfamiliar with the human world to know that glass can cut.

<And he will return to his people a hero,> Ax said. <This will become an oft-repeated and much celebrated chapter in Yeerk history. My name will become legend, synonymous with ineptitude. A brutal fool of an Andalite.>

<Ax, I wouldn't have asked you to do it if it wasn't so important.>

Ax looked at me, fierce hawk eyes glittering. <Important to you, Jake, or to the war effort?>

I didn't answer him.

I wanted to believe it was important to both, but my weary brain couldn't even form the words to convince myself, much less him.

Ax flew back to his woods, muttering something about cleansing rituals.

I flew home and relieved Tobias.

<Everything looks cool, Big Jake,> Tobias said. <So, what's the plan? How do we follow you guys up to the mountains?>

<We leave at noon. We were supposed to leave earlier, but my dad has some stuff to do this morning. I'll meet you all at Cassie's barn at nine to set the plans.>

<OK. Later.>

Tobias flew off.

We were leaving for Grandpa G's cabin in two hours. By the time the others realized I wasn't going to meet them at the barn we'd be long gone.

I was done using my friends on this mission.

I was tired of Marco's doubts and Ax's honour and even Cassie's wary sympathy.

This was my family. My brother, the killer. My father, the target. And me, the fool in the middle.

Just the three of us.

If my brother Tom, in a desperate, last-ditch attempt to save himself, tried to kill my father, then I would morph.

And the last thing my brother would see was me, his brother, his unknown enemy, rear up and destroy him with all the ruthless, savage power that was mine to command.

I had told myself that I would do whatever had to be done, and I would.

Suddenly, I needed to talk to Cassie. And maybe, when it was all over, I would.

Chapter 21

Homer, our dog, had already been taken to Rachel's, where he'd spend the next four days being petted and pampered and played with.

Too bad he and I couldn't have changed places.

And now my father, Tom and I had eight hours of boring motorway driving ahead of us.

Tom sat in the front with my father, sulking and giving monosyllabic answers to my father's forcedly cheerful questions.

I answered a few, but my heart wasn't in it either, and after about fifteen kilometres, my father just stopped trying.

I sat tensely in the back, watching Tom, searching for any signs of Kandrona withdrawal.

Nothing.

Maybe he'd fed last night, in between searching for Chapman.

It wouldn't matter though, because we still wouldn't be home before the three-day limit.

I tried to imagine life without Tom. Without my older brother. I'd be an only child. Marco was an only child. So were Cassie and Tobias.

But I wasn't and I didn't want to be. Saving Tom was the reason I'd agreed to be an Animorph. I hadn't wanted it, any of it. But then I'd learned the Yeerks had taken Tom and made him one of their own.

It was for him that I had endured that first horrifying morph. It was to save him that I had gone down into the Yeerk pool, that unsuspected house of horrors.

I wasn't going to lose Tom to the Yeerks. I had to keep that hope alive.

But I had to keep my father alive, too. The Yeerk in Tom's head was locked in battle with me, though he didn't know it. We were deadly enemies on a field of battle where two innocent people, my brother and my father, stood directly in our line of fire.

After an hour or two, I fell asleep.

Woke up four hours later as we pulled into a rest stop.

We used the toilets. Wolfed down lukewarm hamburgers and stiff, cardboard fries.

Headed back out on the road.

Finally, when I was numb with nerves and cramped from sitting, my father turned the car down a hidden, gravel road.

"We're almost there," he said tiredly.

I sat up.

So did Tom.

Thick forest lined the road, the tree branches seeming to reach for the car. The air was cooler, cleaner, and smelled of dark, moist earth.

A mouse scurried out on to the road in front of us. Sat up, unafraid, and watched as we slowly approached.

"Tseeeer!" A hawk swept down out of nowhere and seized it. Carried it off.

"Survival of the fittest," Tom murmured, his mouth curving into a small, secret smile.

I looked at the side of his head. I looked at his ear, wanting to picture the foul, grey slug that was inside his brain.

Do you have a plan, Yeerk? Are the woods full of your allies? Do the Hork-Bajir lie in wait? Do the Bug fighters hover above us, waiting for the signal?

Or, like me, are you planning on handling this by yourself?

Don't take me on by yourself, Yeerk. You won't win.

Survival of the fittest, Yeerk.

"Finally," my father said, sighing and parking the car. "Everybody out."

My boots crunched noisily on gravel and pine needles. The sound of car doors slamming was both loud and insignificant in the quiet of the woods.

Grandpa G's cabin sat in the middle of a small, grassy clearing surrounded by dark, towering pine trees. There was a well-worn path leading from the front door straight down to the dock at the lake.

Silence. Then, my mother and my grandparents spilled out of the cabin. We were hugged and fussed over, fed and herded back out to the porch to relax.

"It makes me sad to think that Grandpa G isn't here any more," my mother said quietly, watching as the sun set over the lake. "He really loved this place."

"I remember when he came home from the war," my grandfather mused. "He was a different man. He said he wanted nothing but peace after seeing so much."

"Some people just can't deal with the reality of war, I suppose," Tom said offhandedly, earning shocked looks from my parents and grandparents.

"And what would you know about war, Tom?" my grandfather said levelly, like he was trying not to sound as angry as he felt. "I don't recall hearing about your enlistment."

"You're right," Tom said quickly. "That was a stupid thing to say. I suppose I was just thinking

about Grandpa G spending all his time out here, alone."

Everybody relaxed and went on reminiscing.

But I didn't. I just sat and watched and listened.

I had no plan. No plan but to react when Tom struck. I was waiting, playing defence again.

Your move, Yeerk.

Chapter 22

"Why couldn't they have the funeral tomorrow?" Tom said later that night, once we were in the attic bedroom. "I mean, Sunday or Monday, what's the difference?"

"Grandpa G wanted it that way," I answered, looking around the small, dark room. "And besides, Mum said they never bury people on Sunday round here. Sunday is for the wake, Monday for the burial."

"Yeah, well, it's stupid," Tom said, watching me crouch in front of an old chest. "What're you doing?"

"Nothing," I said, lifting a stack of old, dusty books off a small, dark grey leather trunk. "Don't you remember this, Tom? This is Grandpa G's old footlocker."

Tom glanced at it. Then he looked past it, around the room, searching for something to do.

I opened the footlocker, filled with sudden urgency. "Remember back, like, I don't know, when I was ten or so? He showed us his canteen and these pictures of his unit?"

"Maybe," Tom muttered.

"They didn't know whether they were going to freeze or starve or get shot. That's what he said."

Tom rolled his eyes. Indifferent. *Perfectly Tom*, I thought, almost admiring. The Yeerk was keeping up the illusion. Playing the part to perfection.

"Christmas, when they were all homesick in their foxholes, they sang 'Silent Night'. The enemy sang it, too, in German. Far off they heard it. Both sides lonely for their homes. Both sides wishing the war was over."

"Uh-huh."

"Don't you remember how he told us all this, Tom?" I pressed, wanting him to admit he remembered. Wanting, ridiculously, the real Tom inside to push hard enough to break through, just for a minute, and be my totally human brother again.

Tom sighed. "Vaguely. I'm not that big on old war stories."

I lifted out the small box that held Grandpa G's medals, his Silver Star and his Purple Heart. "He was a brave guy. He believed in honour. All that stuff out of old movies. Honour and courage and all."

"Yeah, well, that was all a million years ago," Tom said. "Honour and courage aren't what matters, not in the real world. What matters is whether you win. After you win then you start talking about honour and courage. When you're in battle you do whatever you have to do. Honour and courage and all that? Those are the words you say after you've destroyed all your enemies and anyone else who gets in the way."

"You're wrong," I said flatly.

He rolled his eyes, bored now. "You're a kid." I saw Tom's eyes narrow. "What's this?" He reached into the footlocker and lifted out a cracked leather scabbard. From the sheath he drew a dagger. The blade glittered dully in the dim lamplight. It was a long blade, maybe twenty centimetres or so.

Suddenly, the attic was close and airless.

"It's German," Tom mused, examining it. "It's an old German dagger. Grandpa G must have taken it off a dead soldier as a souvenir. Cool."

"What're you going to do with it?" I asked.

Tom cocked his head and looked at me.

"I mean, you can't take it," I added hurriedly. "It isn't yours."

"Hey, you get the medals, I get the dagger, right?" he said. "It's perfect. You can sit around thinking about honour and bravery and all, and

I get the weapon that gets the job done. Sounds fair to me."

I kept my expression as blank as I could. I, too, was playing a part.

"I'm not taking anything until I talk to Mum and Grandma," I said, carefully putting the medals back in the velvet case and waiting for Tom to do the same with the dagger.

"Well?" I said. "Come on, man, put it back."

"Mum and Grandma," he mocked. "You're still such a kid. You think everything is so simple, don't you? That it's all either right or wrong, black or white. A good guy, a bad guy and nothing in between."

No, Yeerk, I don't. Not any more. I used to. But I've been across the line; I've done things I can't let myself think about. I know all about the shades of grey.

I said, "Sometimes even the good guys do bad things. Doesn't mean there's no difference between good and evil."

"Good and evil," he said with a tired smile. "Strong and weak. That's the reality. Winners and losers."

"The knife, Tom," I said.

He laid it back in the footlocker.

He turned out the light. We crawled into our respective bunks. Our separate foxholes.

Chapter 23

I was cold.

Freezing.

Night.

My feet were solid blocks of ice despite the filthy rags I'd wrapped around my torn boots. My fingers were numb, stiffly clutching my M-1 rifle.

I had a clip and a half of ammo. One grenade. If the Germans came it would be over fast.

I hadn't had a warm meal since. . . Had I ever had a warm meal? Had I ever, ever been warm? Hadn't I always been in this freezing foxhole, this black hole punched in the snow? Hadn't I lived my entire life right here at the edge of the dark forest, shivering, shaking, waiting to hear the scream of incoming shells, waiting to hear the clank-clank-clank of the tanks?

Christmas Eve.

Merry Christmas.

I heard a racking cough from the next foxhole. Matthews. He was from Arkansas. Alabama. One of those places. A southern boy. A kid, one of the last replacements to make it to our unit.

"Hey, kid," I said in a hoarse whisper. "Goose or ham?"

"What?" he gasped between coughs.

"Back home, what does your mum cook for Christmas dinner? Goose or ham?"

For a while he didn't answer. Then, "Ham."

"Yeah? We always have a goose. My mother cooks up a goose."

From a second foxhole, to my right, a voice said, "Don't listen to him, kid. Sarge ain't got no mother."

I think the kid laughed. Hard to tell with the coughing. Pneumonia, most likely. He should be evacuated. But no one was being evacuated. The joke was that even getting yourself killed only got you a three-day pass and then it was back to the line.

"Sarge," he called when the coughing subsided. "Sarge."

"Yeah."

"You write the letter, OK? I know it's the captain's job, but he don't know me. You write the letter."

There was only one letter. The one that

would inform Private Matthews' family that he was among the honoured dead.

I said something rude and obscene. Couldn't have him thinking that way. You start thinking you'll die, maybe you do.

"Tell my mum I did OK," he said.

"Tell her yourself, I'm not the US Mail," I said. "You tell her when you get home."

"Merry Christmas," a bitter voice on my right said.

For a while no one spoke. We listened for the incoming shells. We listened for the tanks. We waited for the crack of a sniper's rifle and the cry of a man dying.

But then the thin, biting air was filled with the sound of voices, ragged at first and then soaring into a harmony that sweetened the night, bringing me home to my family, filling my empty, aching belly and soothing my torn, battered heart.

" 'Silent Night.' "

" 'Holy night,' " Private Matthews whispered, smiling.

"I think I hear the Germans singing, too," I said.

"Yeerks don't sing," Matthews said. Suddenly, he was beside me.

He opened his eyes. Bared his teeth.

And rammed the German dagger straight into my heart.

My eyes snapped open.

Darkness.

I sat up, heart pounding.

Glanced sideways.

The other bed was empty.

I was at Grandpa G's cabin.

Sharing the attic bedroom with my brother.

And it was late. Too late for Tom to be up.

My breath froze in my throat. I rolled over and opened the footlocker.

The dagger was gone.

Chapter 24

I shot out of bed.

Pulled on a sweater and trousers and padded out of the bedroom.

Down the stairs.

The night-light cast a thin, golden glow.

Snoring. Murmuring.

Everyone was still sleeping.

I paused in the main room and looked at the sofabed.

My mother was in it.

My father was gone.

Oh, no! Was I too late? Had I given Tom the exact and perfect chance he'd been waiting for?

I eased open the front door.

Creeee. . .

I went still.

Held my breath.

Nothing.

Squeezed out through the gap and waited in the shadows on the porch.

Listened.

The breeze carried the sound of voices.

There!

My father and Tom were sitting down at the end of the dock, talking and dangling their feet in the water.

My father laughed and gave Tom's shoulders a quick, spontaneous hug.

Tom's sweatshirt bunched up in the back.

Revealing, for a moment, the gleaming dagger wedged in his pocket.

My father didn't notice it. He laughed again and removed his arm.

Tom and my father, sharing a private conversation in the middle of the night.

Tom, the betrayer.

My father, the betrayed.

I had no doubt who'd instigated it.

Tom, apologizing for his bad behaviour. Wanting to talk to my father, man to man.

Lying.

He'd lured my father outside, where no one would hear.

Tom slipped his hand behind him and closed his fingers over the dagger.

Tightened his grip on the handle.

I had to do something.

Fast!

I edged off the porch and took off running, keeping to the deep, dark tree line and morphing as I went.

I didn't care that once I did, Tom would realize I was the enemy.

And that once he knew, I couldn't let him live.

His action, my reaction.

Adrenalin pulsed through my veins.

Drowned out the fluttering panic.

Thick, orange-and-black fur sprouted, rippling over my body. My nose flattened, widened. My senses lit up. Smell! Hearing! Night vision almost as good as an owl's.

I could smell my brother's exultation.

He was excited, anticipating the kill.

Tiger senses. Tiger strength. Tom would be helpless. A boy with a knife against a tiger? Like going up against a tank with a water gun.

I fell forward as my bones ground and remolded into four strong, muscular legs.

Hurry! I shouted silently, stumbling as my feet widened and my toenails curved into deadly claws.

But I was still only halfway to the dock when Tom withdrew the glittering dagger.

Chapter 25

CCCRRRRAAAACCCKKKK!

The sharp sound split the night.

My father and Tom looked up in shock as the wooden dock tilted and collapsed with a screech.

They scrabbled to hold on, but the planks were an accordion being squeezed. The entire dock was being folded back on itself by some massive force.

Tom and my father both slipped into the water.

"Hey!" my father shouted, going under.

He bobbed back up, gasped, thrashed and went down again.

I stopped dead in the shadows, surprised, amazed, waiting to see what was happening.

My dad could swim like a fish. Why was he surfacing and going back under?

"Glug," he croaked, surfacing several metres away from the ruined dock and almost immediately disappearing again.

It was almost as if something was pulling him down and towing him away from Tom. . .

Tom was frantic, splashing and swinging around in the water, not trying to save my father, just trying to keep him in sight. Why? So he could watch him die? So he could catch up with him and use the dagger?

Silent anger roared in my ears.

My fur rippled and stood on end.

My still-human mouth tightened into a snarl.

I moved forward again.

"Gak," my father burbled, surfacing another ten metres away from the dock.

Tom swung around in the water, searching for him.

Suddenly, a fin broke the lake's surface behind Tom.

Shark? I thought blankly. *Shark in a mountain lake?*

No, not a shark.

A dolphin!

Before I could move, the fin sliced through the water and something slammed straight into Tom's back.

"Oof!" Tom arched, eyes wide with surprise,

and shot forward, ploughing facedown in the rippling lake.

He didn't move after that.

The fin — no, there were more than one — the fins slipped soundlessly below the surface.

"Tom! Tom, are you all right?!" my father yelled, clambering up on to shore. He'd been dragged some twenty metres down the lake and was staggering back through the thick, vine-covered underbrush.

Tom was floating facedown, motionless in the water.

My father would never get there in time to save him.

I could. The tiger can swim. I could save him.

But I didn't move. Frozen. Brain locked around the simple fact that if Tom died he would, at last, be free. That if the Yeerk died I would have had my revenge. That we would be safer, stronger, freer with the Controller named Tom dead and gone.

Didn't know what to do.

<Jake! Demorph!> a voice ordered. <You're in the open. Demorph!>

I obeyed, glad for once to take orders rather than give them. Relieved to have the decision made for me.

The others had followed me to the cabin. They'd backed me up even though I'd said not to. They'd taken the decision out of my hands.

I stepped forward. My feet had remoulded to human.

I stood up. My fur had disappeared.

Tom would drown unless I saved him.

Saving him might still mean my father's death.

Help me! I wanted to scream. *Tell me what to do!*

The lake water rippled. Surged.

And suddenly Tom's limp, unconscious body was skimming across the water like a surfboard, being pushed rapidly towards shore.

I ran to the water's edge. My reflection in the moonlit ripples was human.

Panting, I dragged Tom's body up on to the land.

Flipped him over.

Water streamed from his still face.

His right leg flopped and twisted at a crazy, sickening, unnatural angle.

"Help," I croaked, leaping to my feet. "*Help!*"

Tom groaned. Coughed.

He gagged and barfed up buckets of smelly lake water.

"Don't move," I babbled, trying to hold him still as he thrashed. Something was wrong with his leg. There was a hinge where there shouldn't be one. "I think your leg is broken."

"Jake!" my father shouted, staggering up. His clothes were sagging, sopping and ripped,

and he was covered with dark, slimy mud. "Is Tom all right?"

"No," I said, shaking my head. "Someone had better call an ambulance. Dad, hurry!"

My father ran to the cabin.

I looked down at Tom. Inside his head was a killer. He'd almost killed my father.

But what I saw, the eyes I looked into, those belonged to my big brother.

I settled into the mud next to him.

His face was white and tight with shock, his eyes filled with dark agony. His teeth were chattering and tears leaked down into his hair.

"Get out of here, midget," he gasped, writhing. "Get out of here and leave me alone!"

"No," I said, moving closer. "I . . . don't think so."

And I didn't until I heard a deep, pulsing THWOK THWOK THWOK and a medevac helicopter dropped out of the starry sky and swept Tom away.

Chapter 26

"OK, honey. You, too."

My father hung up the phone and sighed. He ran a hand through his rumpled hair, then turned to face the sea of anxious faces.

"Well?" I asked.

"Your mum says they medevaced Tom all the way back to the hospital back home," my father said, plopping down in a chair. "It seems he has a complex break and our hospital's the only one in the area equipped to deal with it."

"No kidding," I said, not at all surprised.

Of course: back home. Back where there were plenty of Controllers around to make absolutely certain Tom would have access to the Yeerk pool's lifesaving Kandrona rays.

"He's in some pain and he'll be laid up for a

while, but at least he's gonna be OK," my father said thickly. He reached over and hugged me. "Thank God you got there in time to save him, Jake."

"I didn't save him," I said. "He drifted into shore. I just grabbed him and hauled him out of the water."

"And saved him," my father insisted, releasing me. "I was really scared tonight, Jake. I don't ever want to lose either one of you."

"Me, either," I said.

And we had come so close. A dagger half-drawn. A tiger running.

"Well, I need a cup of coffee," my father said.

"I'll make it," my grandmother said.

"Make one for me, too, please," my grandfather called after her.

"First thing tomorrow morning, I'm going to call whoever built that dock and read them the riot act," my father said. "And then I want to talk to somebody about the undertow or the current or whatever it was that dragged me down that lake. It's dangerous!"

"Yeah. Um, look, I'll be right back, OK?" I said. "Need some fresh air." I slipped out of the door and into the fading darkness.

I stood for a moment listening, but it was no use.

Human hearing is so limited.

I spread my hands like, *Well?*

<Over here, Jake,> Tobias called from a thick stand of pine trees.

I walked over and met them in the shadows.

Without my asking, they told me how they'd done it.

How Tobias had kept endless watch and sounded the alarm when Tom and my father exited the cabin.

How Cassie had quickly morphed to whale and struggled through a shallow, nerve-wracking six metres of water to ram the dock, praying she wouldn't be beached before she got there.

How Rachel and Ax had morphed into dolphins, rammed Tom, broken his leg, and dragged my father to safety.

I wanted to say a lot.

Like how they'd saved my family.

My sanity.

"Thanks," I said.

"Hey, don't mention it," Rachel said fliply. "We needed a holiday, anyway."

<We have spent time exploring that decrepit architectural structure riddled with rodents and assorted wildlife,> Ax said, turning an eye stalk towards the abandoned hunting lodge across the lake. <We discovered several extremely large spiders.>

"And rats. Don't leave out the rats," Cassie said with a laugh.

<Personally, I had fun,> Tobias offered.

"That's because you got to eat like a pig," Rachel said.

They were trying too hard.

"Where's Marco?" I said.

Cassie shrugged. "He didn't know if you'd want to see him right away. Thought you might need some time to calm down or whatever."

"Come on out, Marco."

He stepped into view from behind a tree. He looked a little leery. Which, given the way I'd treated him, was not surprising.

"Hey, Big Jake."

"Marco. This had to be your plan."

"Pretty much."

"Yeah. Well. Good plan."

"Thanks. Couldn't have done it without the Chee," Marco said, shrugging like it was nothing. "They're the ones who piloted the medevac helicopter and insisted on taking Tom back home. Without them, all we would have had was a kid with a busted leg out in the middle of the woods."

"Tom's back home. Alive. My dad's alive. Crisis past. I should have thought of it myself. Tom, injured, had the perfect excuse for not coming on this trip. I should have seen that."

Marco shrugged. "Yeah, well. . ."

"I was too close to it," I said. "You were right. I was too close to see things clearly."

Marco didn't argue. He didn't gloat, either. I guess we each have our strengths and weaknesses. Marco's strength is the ability to see the way to the goal, even when it means disregarding consequences and feelings and basic right and wrong.

He'd seen this solution when I missed it.

I took Marco's arm and drew him away from the others. To where they wouldn't hear.

"You're my best friend, Marco. If you ever again tell me I'm losing it, getting too involved, can't lead—"

"You'll kick my butt?" he interrupted with a grin.

"No. I'll listen. I'll listen. Then I'll kick your butt."

He laughed. I laughed. What can I say? Marco and I have been friends for ever.

We started to rejoin the others. I stopped him. "Marco?"

"What?"

"This whole plan worked because Tom came outside and made himself vulnerable. What would have happened if he hadn't?"

Marco didn't look at me.

"You had to keep me from blowing it at all costs," I pressed. "You had to preserve the security of the group and keep me alive. Those were your top priorities."

He nodded.

"So, what if you hadn't been in time? What if Tom had managed to kill my father?"

"It was pretty clear, after I thought about it, that if Tom killed your father you'd lose it," Marco said coolly. "Like a chess game: Tom takes your father, you take Tom. You'd have gone after Tom, exposing yourself and us. Game over. So we couldn't let that happen. Your dad had to survive for you to survive. The one expendable piece was Tom. But if anything was going to happen to Tom it would have to look natural, not like an Animorph had been involved, and not like you had been involved. It would have to be done very carefully. So, if it came down to that—"

"No," I said softly. I shook my head. I didn't want to know.

For a while neither of us said anything. I just let it sink in.

You know what Marco and I used to talk about? Whether Batman could beat Spider-Man. Whether Sega was better than Nintendo. Whether some girl would rather go out with him or me.

And now. . .

"What are we, any more, Marco? What has happened to us?"

He didn't answer. I didn't expect him to. We both knew what had happened.

"I better get back inside," I said.

"Yeah. And we need to head home. We hitched a ride on a cattle lorry getting here. We're hoping for something less fragrant for the return trip."

I went back towards the cabin.

Chapter 27

My mum was back the next day. It was Sunday, the day for Grandpa G's wake, and then we had his funeral on Monday.

The local Veterans' Association came and brought a bugler, who played a slow, mournful Taps.

The other old soldiers took the folded American flag off the casket and gave it to my grandmother, Grandpa G's daughter.

She and the worn, grizzled men looked at each other for a long, quiet moment as if sharing a memory, a lifetime of experiences only they could understand.

I understood it, though.

Maybe not their war, but ours. Because now we're the ones out on the battle lines. The ones who fight and bleed, succeed and fail, win and lose.

We're the ones with the nightmares and the old souls.

I know what Grandpa G meant now.

He only talked about the war twice, at least to me. Once, when he opened his footlocker. And the other, that day, long ago, when we'd sat on the dock.

When my war ends, if I survive, I probably won't talk about it much, either.

As far as experiences go, once will be enough.

We each laid a rose on the casket as we left.

It wasn't a big funeral, but everyone there cried. Anyway, I did.

When we got back to the cabin we called the hospital and talked to Tom. He was doing fine.

Everything was back the way it had been. My brother still lived. So did the enemy inside him. It had all been a pointless battle. No one had wanted it, no one had profited. Everyone had suffered: Chapman, Ax, Tom, Marco and some guy who just wanted his parking space back. And me.

But we'd all survived, and in war any time you wake up to see the sunrise it's a victory.

My folks and I drove home together on Tuesday.

I sat in the front seat with my dad while my mum dozed in the back.

Dad let me choose the radio station and told me for only about the ten millionth time how much better the music was "in his day". We had burgers for lunch and my mum told us both for only about the ten millionth time that we ate too much saturated fat. We pulled off to witness the "World's Largest Ball of Twine!" You know, except for all the other "World's Largest" twine balls.

Small, simple things, but good ones.

We talked about Grandpa G and then about other stuff.

Normal stuff.

The ride always seems shorter on the way home.

Tom had dropped the German dagger in the water when he'd been knocked off the pier. I suppose it had sunk to the bottom of the lake.

I could have retrieved it, probably. I didn't.

But I had Grandpa G's medals in my pocket. My grandmother had given them to me. She said Grandpa G wanted me to have them.

I always knew he'd been a hero in the war. That he had medals and all. And I'd wondered why he didn't put them up in a display case, show them off for all the world to see.

But I was a little wiser, now.

Medals aren't so simple for the people who earn them. Every time Grandpa G had looked at those medals he'd thought about the things that had happened, the things he'd seen others do, the things he'd done himself.

I know he was proud of being brave, proud of doing his best for his country. But I also know why the medals were in a pouch, in a footlocker, in an attic, kept far out of sight.

Someday maybe there'll be medals for those who fought the war against the Yeerks.

I'll need to buy a footlocker.

Don't miss

ANIMORPHS®

32 The Separation

I stood up. Looked around. Not three metres away was this guy named Bailey. I don't know if that's his first name or last name.

"What do you want?" I demanded.

"Nothing." He shrugged.

I glared.

He blushed.

"Looking good, Rachel."

"What?"

"That leotard and all. You're looking good."

I was wearing my morphing outfit. It seemed OK for a trip around the rocks.

"Of course I look good," I snapped. "I almost always do. You have something else to say?"

I guess that threw him. He shrugged.

"Looking good," he repeated. "Looking *real* good."

"I think we've been over that," I said. "Yes, I am good-looking. Yes, I have great hair. Yes, I have a great body. Now go away."

"You are so stuck-up!"

"That's right, I am. Now you know the difference between good looks and a good personality."

He left. I waited till he was back with a group of his friends. I scanned the other direction along the shoreline. A family with two kids, two little boys. They were coming my way but I'd have time to morph before they got close.

I began to morph.

First I shrank. Smaller and smaller. Puddles and pools rushed up towards me. A shower of spray hit me and all of a sudden it wasn't refreshing, it was scary. The force of the water nearly knocked me off my feet.

Which was easier to do since my feet were disappearing. My thighs grew thick. My arms thickened as well, forming chubby cones.

Arm, arm, leg, leg. And here was the gross part: My head was morphing to become the fifth leg. It turns out starfish don't exactly have heads. They have a mouth more or less in the middle, a bunch of wiggly little feet that look like suckers, and the five big cone legs.

That's about it for a starfish. A cockroach,

by comparison, is a model of sophisticated design.

I went blind. Totally. No eyes at all.

It occurred to me to wonder how exactly I expected to find an earring when I couldn't see, but I assumed the starfish would have other compensating senses.

Nope. Not really.

It could feel. It could sort of smell. It could scoot around on its many tiny little feet. If it happened, mostly by accident, to crawl on to something tasty I guess it could eat it. But that was pretty much it for the starfish.

Well, I told myself, I might be able to feel the earring.

I motored my many little feet. Down, down, slithering down wet rock.

<OK, this is stupid. An unfamiliar morph in a hole in the rock. Not your brightest move, Rachel.>

Then my foot — one of them, anyway — touched something thin and hard and round.

Amazing! I had stumbled on to the earring. It took me another ten minutes to get my useless little mouth to grab the earring. I headed back up. At least I hoped it was up.

I climbed up over the lip of the pool, out into relative dryness. I focused my mind on morphing and began to—

WHAM!

Something hit me. Hit me hard.

The starfish didn't have much in the way of pain sensors but I still knew, the starfish knew, deep down, that it was very, very badly hurt.

I tried to make sense of it all. But all I knew for sure was this: I had been able to count to five on my starfish legs.

Now I could only count to two.

I was cut in half!

<Aaaahhhh!> I yelled.

Panic, blind panic hit me.

I was cut in half! I had to die. Had to! There was no way. . .

But I was still alive.

Demorph!

That was it. Yeah. Demorph. Yeah, yeah, change back. Oh, lord! I was chopped in half!

I focused. Focused on the image of myself, my real self.

Demorph, Rachel. Demorph and live!

I began to change.

Eyes! I could see!

Rocks, all around me. But sky above. Blue sky and white, fluffy clouds! I could see!

Tiny little blue eyes sticking out of a starfish leg.

I continued demorphing. I dragged myself up, centimetre by centimetre and peeked carefully over the lip of rock.

Half a starfish lay unchanged in the tidal

pool. Two legs and a chunk of a third. And an earring.

I caught a glimpse of the family, the two boys. One of them had a bucket. And a shiny new steel spade.

He'd been the one who had cut me.

He'd been the one who'd almost killed me.

Rotten, filthy little brat!

"I'll kill him!" I said. "Kill him! Kill the filthy little creep!" Morph to grizzly bear and tear him apart! No. No. Not the kid. Bailey! His fault. He delayed me, otherwise it would have all worked perfectly.

I stood up.

"Bailey!" I screamed against the crashing waves, shaking my clenched fists in rage. "I'll kill you! I'll kill you! I'll murder you!"

He heard nothing, of course, over the sound of the waves. And that was a good thing.

It occurred to me that killing Bailey was probably an overreaction.

But just the same, it would teach him a lesson.

Chapter 3

I finished demorphing. It was a terrifying, hideous experience. But the alternative was even worse. I demorphed in a total, like, panic! I wasn't even thinking, just screaming inside my mind, screaming and begging for it to be over.

I rose from the rocks, so grateful to be fully human, so relieved. I saw the others, far off. I caught a glimpse of a blonde girl, running away. I didn't recognize her.

Had she seen me?

The earring! There it was, stuck between my toes. Oh, good. It was a cool earring, really. Not like some of the stuff your parents might buy you. You know parents. Right?

Anyway. . .

I ran back to the others, too.

I needed to be with, like, people. I needed to have familiar voices and faces around me.

So scared!

I was shaking. I was going to go on shaking for ever.

Was I insane? Why had I done something as reckless as morphing a starfish?

And. . .

And why had I been so mean to Bailey? All he'd wanted to do was compliment me. He just wanted to say he thought I was pretty; why had I been so, like, harsh and stuck-up?

Later I would have to find the time and the right way to apologize. Maybe if I went out on a date with him—

Oh, wait. No. That would hurt Tobias's feelings. I was sure it would.

I was supposed to go flying with Tobias after school. We did that a lot, me and Tobias. Tobias is a *nothlit*. That's an Andalite word for a person who stays in morph past the two-hour limit.

Tobias was trapped now, as a red-tailed hawk.

They are very scary birds.

I mean, he's a boy, really. A very sweet boy. Like Bailey. Only I could kiss Bailey, couldn't I? Yes. I could. It would be nice.

Nice kissing Tobias, too. If he was in human morph.

They were both cute. They were both nice. Sweet. Gentle. Kind. All those good things.

Only, Tobias killed mice and ate them. Which was not all that sweet, really.

Oh, well.

"Are you OK, Rachel?" a girl named Dahlia asked.

"Oh! Does it show?" I asked, pressing my hands against my face.

"Forget it," Dahlia said, looking disgusted. "Why would I try and be nice to you? All I get is sarcasm."

"Oh, Dahlia," I said, reaching out for her. "I'm sorry you feel that way. Really! I want to be friends. I really, really do."

Dahlia made a face. "You know, you were always stuck-up, Rachel, but lately you're just this total, like, witch."

She turned away and I felt hot tears flood my eyes. Why would she say that about me? I was being sincere. I really did want to be friends.

We all walked towards the bus. Boy, was that ever a welcome sight after all I'd been through!

I climbed aboard and got into my seat. My shoes were under the seat. My outer clothing was in my backpack. I pulled a sweater on.

I wish they had seat belts on buses, don't you?

"That's a cute sweater," this girl named Elizabeth said. She was sitting next to me.

"Thanks. I got it at Abercrombie? It's, like, on sale? Forty-two fifty marked down to twenty-seven ninety-five."

"No way! Are you going to the mall after school?"

OK, so I should go straight to meet Tobias after school. That's what I should do. I had promised. Only. . .

But did I want to go be with Tobias? Or did I want to go shopping?

Would Cassie go shopping with me? She didn't like shopping very much. But she might go. I could, like, ask her. But what about Elizabeth? She'd asked me already. Only I didn't really like Elizabeth all that much, and I did like Cassie. Only Cassie might not want to go shopping.

And Tobias! He'd be so sad if I didn't show up.

But if I showed up he'd, like, want me to morph and all, and it was so scary, flying, way up in the air with nothing holding you up — oh my Gawd! I couldn't believe I ever did it!

"So?" Elizabeth asked.

"What?" I asked.

She shrugged. "Forget it."

Chapter 4

I hooked up with Tobias at his meadow.

He saw me coming and swept down out of the sky, fierce, wild, a thing of dangerous beauty.

<Hi, Rachel. Hear anything from Jake about the mission?>

"I haven't seen Jake. Don't worry, he'll get word to us if there's killing to be done. Ha! Anti-Morphing Ray! You have to admire the Yeerks: they never stop trying. They never stop trying to take us down! Now, let's fly!"

I began to morph. My bird-of-prey morph is the bald eagle. It's only fitting. Nothing against hawks, but eagles are bigger, more dangerous. I'm sure if Tobias had it to do all over again he'd get trapped as an eagle.

The bad part of morphing to eagle is the shrinking. You get smaller. A lot smaller, and your first thought is, *Hey, smaller is weaker and no way I want to be weaker!*

But then you feel your weak, useless human lips harden and push out and out, forming the wicked, yellow, downturned, ripping, tearing eagle beak, and you think, *Hah! Smaller, yes, but not weaker!*

You watch the feather pattern as it draws across your flesh, and feel the strange, distant itching when those patterns become three-dimensional.

Your bones hollow and shrink, your arms twist and rotate, your insides slosh and melt and re-form into inhuman organs.

Your feet, your soft, stubby, awkward human feet melt like wax and then harden into talons.

As wonderful as the eagle's beak is, the talons are the true weapons. So powerful they can grab and hold a young lamb. They can snatch and squeeze and penetrate flesh and organ and skull and brain.

Eyes that can see a flea hopping on a rabbit's back from fifty metres away! Ears that can hear a mouse sneeze! Reflexes like lightning!

A wonderful creature. A natural predator. Raptor! The killer from the sky!

I wondered if I could take Tobias in an

air-to-air fight. He was more manoeuvrable and experienced. But I had the brute power.

Well, another day, maybe. Tobias was a true warrior. The right sort of partner for me. Someone who understood that—

<Ready?> Tobias asked. <Come on, there are some sweet thermals coming up off the road today with this sun.>

I flapped my wings. I turned to catch a slight headwind. My wings filled and I soared.

Up and up and up we went. Tobias was right! The thermals off the road, the heat boiling up from sunbaked concrete and car engines was like a lift beneath our wings.

Up and up!

We were gods! We could have flown to the sun! Humans in their cars were puny, flaccid, paltry, limited creatures, far, far beneath us.

Five hundred metres up there was a delicious, cool breeze that we used to rocket us forward, zooming over factories and car parks, over meadows and streams and woods.

Then. . .

Far, far below, so far no human could ever have spotted it, a school of fish, fast and silver, in a stream decorated with garlands of white water.

I spilled air, tucked my wings back, and dived.

The rush!

The thrill!

I was an eagle being an eagle. Pure raptor! Pure rapture!

That struck me as a good thought. <Tobias!> I cried. <Pure raptor, pure rapture! Ah HAH!>

<Rachel, what are you doing?>

Down, down, down, so fast the wind was a hurricane over my wings. Then, slow just a bit, use my tail to aim, to change my trajectory as I singled out a single, particular victim.

My eagle's eyes, adapted by nature for seeing through water, filtering out the glare, saw it all: six fish, six trout, all unaware, and one, one I chose, would die!

You! You will never live to chase another fisherman's lure! I have chosen you to die!

I raked my talons forward.

I flared my wings.

A splash!

The sudden, lovely feeling of my talons striking firm, cold flesh.

Strike!

I squeezed and talons sank deep. The fish, only now recognizing its doom, squirmed. *Helpless! I am the eagle! You cannot resist me!*

I fluttered, carrying the spasming creature over to the bank. I landed on a flat rock. I steadied myself with one talon and held my victim with the other.

I looked into his stupid, terrified eyes, and

with my razor beak I ripped him open. Scales flew. Fish guts spilled.

I buried my beak, up to the eyes in the cool, squirming flesh. I felt the heart still beating.

I ate the fish, ripping big chunks and gulping them down.

<Rachel! What are you doing? Did you lose control of the morph?>

<What am I doing? I am eating this fish. He's mine! Get back! He's my kill. MY kill!>

I ate the heart. Then, it stopped beating.